Lock Down Publications and Ca$h Presents

I0664167

ONCE YOU GO GANGSTA

Champagne & Hallowpoints

Written By
COREY ROBINSON

First Edition 2025

Printed in the United States of America

This is a work of fiction. Names, characters, places, and incidents either are products of the author's imagination or are used fictitiously. Any similarity to actual events or locales or persons, living or dead, is entirely coincidental.

Lock Down Publications
P.O. Box 944
Stockbridge, GA 30281
www.lockdownpublications.com

Like our page on Facebook: Lock Down Publications
www.facebook.com/lockdownpublications.ldp

Stay Connected with Us!

Text **LOCKDOWN** to 22828 to stay up-to-date with new releases, sneak peaks, contests and more…

Like our page on Facebook:
Lock Down Publications

Join Lock Down Publications/The New Era Reading Group

Visit our website:
www.lockdownpublications.com

Follow us on Instagram:
Lock Down Publications

Email Us: We want to hear from you!

Chapter 1

"So you sure you ain't got nothing you want to enlighten me on? 'Cause honestly, you look like you got a lot to say," Monty threatened the man he held captive.

"Fuck you, mane. I ain't telling your ass shit. You can sit there and threaten me all you want, but I don't give a damn about you killing me. Shit, you probably gone kill me regardless if I talk or not. But guess what? I signed on for this, and I ride for mine all the way. Hell, at least everyone will know I died a mufuckin G."

"A G, huh? So you willing to give your life for a mufucka who wouldn't do the same for you? Hmm. That's really impressive." Monty nodded slowly, but in a subtle, threatening manner.

"Well then, I guess I'm just an impressive ass nigga. I took an oath when I signed up for this street shit, so you can try all you want, but you can't even put a dent in the loyalty I hold for my people. You might as well save your time and energy for those weak ass punks who fall for stuff like this, 'cause I ain't the mufuckin one." The captive showed no fear.

"Ya know? You talk a lot of big boy shit, but we gone find out if you can back it up. I want to see just how much heart a nigga like you really has. Go 'head and handle your business, fellas. Let's see how tough this mufucka really is."

Monty leaned back in the plush leather chair with his legs crossed one over the other. He sipped on the glass of sparkling champagne while his AR-15 sat on the table next to him. The blunt he held between his fingers filled the room

4

with clouds of smoke every time he took a pull. Monty watched closely while four of his goons roughed up the nigga who had been putting in work on his block. Monty just knew he worked for the opps; he just didn't know which one. He hadn't been sure just how much information the man would be willing to give up, but so far, it had been none, and no matter how many punches and kicks were thrown at him, the mufucka remained solid. He was the type of soldier Monty would have liked to have on his team. It was too bad he worked for the other side and not him.

At one time in Monty's life, the scene before him would have fucked with his mind really hard, but he had grown into a different man, and it was now his new normal. Monty thought nothing of seeing a man get beat down and tortured until the life drained from his soul. That shit meant nothing to him, and when it would be him delivering the punishment, it brought him pure joy. It made his dick so hard that he would have to go and fuck something afterwards.

Killing mufuckas wasn't his only hobby. Monty liked to stack paper and showboat. He also liked to fuck as many hos as he could. He didn't even care who they belonged to, because a mufucka wasn't going to tell him where to stick his dick.

He seemed to have a different bitch on his jock every other week, but he told himself that when the right one came along, he was going to chill and settle down. However, she had yet to come into his life.

Montana Hardy had been raised by a single mother with a strong Christian faith, while his father, Montel, sat inside a federal prison cell. Hoping to keep him from following in his father's footsteps, she did her best to raise him right. She even made him attend church at least three times a week, but right when Monty was about to go deep in his Bible, his mother died from a sudden heart attack. Monty found it hard to understand why the God she served didn't spare her, especially after all the time she had invested in him. It made

Monty so angry, he threw his Bible in the trash. He also pushed the church and everything it had taught him to the side.

Monty had only been fifteen when his mother passed away, and to keep him from becoming state property, a family member he never knew he had stepped up. Monty's uncle Taboo was a small-time marijuana dealer on the other side of town. Taboo was his father's older brother, and Monty wondered why his mother had never mentioned him before. However, she never really talked to him about his own father either.

Taboo had never slipped up and made any children of his own, and he wasn't too keen on raising someone else's, but the promise of a monthly check from the welfare department quickly changed his mind. Once Taboo signed his name on the dotted line, he walked away. Monty would be on his own and would have to find a way to fend for himself.

Monty's mother had never told him about the life his father lived, so he didn't know he had the blood of a gangster pumping through his veins. He had been content growing up with just one parent, so he never questioned anything else. Monty's mother provided everything he needed. It wasn't much, but it kept clothes on Monty's back and food in his stomach. The one thing she never taught him, though, was how to survive in the streets.

Monty hit the block for the first time in his life and ran into a corner boy who went by the name of Chance. He had earned the name due to the fact that he was willing to try anything once. Chance wasn't afraid of anything or anyone, and everybody knew it, so when he took Monty under his wing, the entire hood knew not to fuck with him.

Chance taught Monty how to cook, cut, weigh, package, and sell the cocaine he pushed out in the streets, and Monty caught on as if he'd been doing it all his life. Being a drug dealer came naturally, but when it came to busting caps in a mufucka, that was another story. It took Monty months of training before he could hit the mark, but once he got it, he never missed again. Chance rewarded him with his very own .45, and it made Monty feel even more powerful. Once Chance felt like he was ready, he sent Monty out on his own. Seven years later, Monty formed his own crew and became a force to be reckoned with. He instilled fear in the hood, and nobody dared to try him—except, of course, the opps.

"Enough! You pussy-ass mufuckas over there swingin' and workin' up a sweat for nothing. I guess I'm a have to get up and show you how it's done."

Monty shouted, stopping his goons from the useless beating they had been giving out. He stood from his chair with the champagne glass still in his hand. Monty put the rim of the glass to his mouth and emptied its contents, then set it on the table. He picked up the AR-15.

Monty walked over to his goons and filled all four of them with bullets. He knew not to ever leave a witness behind, no matter who they were or who they worked for. Chance taught him that many great names got caught up because of the people that worked for them, and he should never consider it a loss. Also, there were plenty of other niggas who wanted to join Monty's set, so he definitely wouldn't be lacking in soldiers.

The man who sat strapped in the chair jumped at the sound of the rifle being fired. He looked up at Monty through black, swollen eyes and smiled. The blood slid down his cheeks like tears, dropping little red dots on his clothes. He breathed heavily as he spoke, and although he tried to mask his fear, Monty could tell that he was scared as a mufucka.

"I—I told you mu, mufuck, mufucka. I'm a ride, ride for mine. They—they don't make, make soldiers like me, like me no more. Ain't no, no place in the game for a rat, and you—you, out of all people, got—gotta respect that. I—I think that's why, why you just shot and killed, killed your own people. It's—it's a shame you can't trust niggas these days. Now, now do what you gotta do, so, so I can rest in peace."

"Now see, that would be a little too easy. See, a nigga like me, I respect loyalty, and because of that, I'm a give you a chance. And if you actually make it out of here, I need you to deliver a message for me. Tell whoever it is that you work for to stay outta my way, because I own these streets, and I don't take kindly to mufuckas trespassing on my turf. My momma didn't bear me any siblings, so I never learned how to share. This will be their only warning."

"Yeah, I'll deliver that message, but—but I can't promise anyone will listen."

"Well, for your sake and theirs, you better make them. And just so you know, I'm about to burn this bitch down. My suggestion to you is to try and make it out alive, because if you don't, then that means my message won't get delivered, and then, I'm really gonna be pissed off. Might even be so pissed that I'll have to go and visit your family. Wouldn't want that to happen. Now would you?"

"Come on, Monty. My, my family ain't got shit to do with, with what I got goin' on in the streets. I—I'ma spread that, that message you gave me, I—I promise. Just as soon as you, you untie me and let me go."

"Now you see. That's where you got it all wrong. I'm not untying you. That's the part you gone have to figure out all on your own. I mean, you did figure out how to trespass on my turf, so you should be a pro at it by now. Know what I mean?"

Monty lifted the assault rifle and hit the man in the head, splitting it open. He then turned around, picked up his empty glass and the remainder of his blunt, and reached down to grab a gallon canister of gasoline. Monty held up the canister and smiled. He had planned to douse the entire room and then changed his mind. He thought it would be better to pour it in the places that mattered and then make a trail on his way out the door. When Monty stepped outside, he stood still for a moment so he could enjoy the cool breeze the darkness had brought, then he lit a match.

Monty felt like he had given the nigga a fair chance to survive. He had claimed to be a soldier, so Monty figured that if he wanted to live bad enough, he would find a way to free himself from the chains that bound him. Monty would never know one way or the other, and frankly, he didn't give a damn. The opps would get the message either way, because he would continue to knock off their men until they listened.

Monty pulled up to his massive estate and parked in the circular driveway. He was still young, but he was proud of the things he had accomplished so far. But the gangsta in him couldn't help but wonder just how long he'd be able to enjoy the fruits of his labor. Monty knew that the lifestyle he had chosen could cost him his life in the blink of an eye, but he wasn't going to let that stop him, because he wasn't ready to pull out, and quite possibly, never would be.

It wasn't until Monty heard the knock on his window that he came out of his thoughts. He had forgotten about the bitch he had left in his bed when he went out to handle his business earlier that day. Her name was Bella, and she had to be the finest Latina he had ever seen. Monty couldn't resist her fat ass, slim waist, perky breasts, and most of all, her head game. The bitch was good at what she done and had sucked Monty's dick so good, it brought tears to his eyes. It hadn't been the first time he'd gotten good head, but when he was in Bella's mouth, he couldn't remember anyone else before her. The fact that the pussy was good, too, was a plus. Bella was the complete package, but unfortunately, she would never be the woman he could settle down with. When they were together, Monty enjoyed Bella's company, but the way she sucked and fucked him was the same way she did it for all the other niggas in the game.

Monty looked out his window and licked his lips as soon as he saw her. Bella stood there with her hands on her hips as if she had an attitude. The shit was sexy to Monty and caused him to rock up instantly. The bottom of her breasts peeked out from the edge of the tank top, while the cool night breeze caused her fat nipples to harden and push through the fabric. The baby blue mesh thong revealed the outline of her pussy and caused Monty to rub on his manhood, and then he opened his door.

"Dayum, Bella, you doin' the damn thing, baby. If a nigga knew he was comin' home to all that, he would've been home sooner."

"Ah, Monty, baby, you say that always, but you still go for so long. Yo should no want to leave all this, unless, of course, you have other women to tend to. Bella no like to share."

"Now tell me what I'ma do with another woman when I got all of this in front of me?"

"You speak so well of me, papi, but you no show it. I no like it when you're away for so long. Bella misses you so much."

"Oh yeah? Bella be missin' me? Why don't you go ahead and show me how much, 'cause right now, all that you talkin', sounds like a bunch of bullshit."

"Mmm, papi. Bella would never bullshit you."

Bella instantly dropped to her knees in front of him. She didn't care that they were outside in the driveway. She only wanted to do whatever she could to please him in hopes of securing a permanent spot by his side, but little did she know, she was wasting her time. Monty didn't look at Bella as wifey material, and he never would. She was just something wet to slide into, and that was all she would ever be.

"Damn, Bella baby, you sure know how to make a nigga forget all his worries. That shit feels damn good, but I wanna bust off while I'm in that pussy."

Without releasing Monty's manhood from her mouth, Bella looked up at him. She loved it when he talked nasty to her, and it caused her to suck even harder. Once she made him cum in her mouth, she swallowed and smiled.

"Bella really, really likes you, papi, and will let you beat this kitty up right here and right now. She's been cryin' for you all day, but now, she's ready to purr."

Bella reached down and patted her fat mound and winked at Monty. He had to give her credit, the bitch was an expert in seduction, but Monty was no weak-minded mufucka. When he made the comment about busting a nut inside of her, he meant with a condom on. Bella, along with many other hos, had tried to get him to raw-dog it, but thankfully, Monty thought with his brain and not his dick. Chance had made sure to instill in him the consequences he could face if he didn't protect his package.

"Oh, don't worry, I'ma beat that thang up all right, but it won't be out here. It's gone have to wait 'til we on the inside of the house, you know that's where I keep my condoms. Shiit, the last thing I need to do is slip up. Know what I mean?"

"Come on, Monty, you know me is on that little pill thing. You no have to worry about any surprises from me."

"Hell nah. That little pill don't mean shit. Besides, I don't even know if you take it every day or not, so I wear a condom, or you get no dick, you decide, 'cause I'm cool either way."

"Fine then. I'm going back inside. You just better hope my pussy is still wet when you get there."

Monty shook his head at Bella's words and watched her walk away with a straight attitude. He instantly had regrets about letting her chill at his place for the weekend. Monty had never been desperate to get up in some pussy, even though he liked it very much. There damn sure wasn't a shortage of it, so he could stand to pass some up if he needed to, but he was saving up his baby mankind seeds for the right one. If a bitch couldn't accept that, then they could move the fuck on.

Monty suddenly felt as if he had given Bella the wrong impression, and she thought she had him right where she wanted him. But he was going to show her that she didn't. Monty would go ahead and let her stay there that night, but it would be the last one. After that, he would take her ass right back where he got her from, and until he found the right one, Bella would be the last female he brought home. Monty decided that the best thing for him to do was camp out at the Holiday Inn for the rest of the night. He hadn't been in the mood to be fucked up with a bitch anyway. He hoped that Bella got a good night's sleep in his bed, because it would be her last one. The next day, he planned on telling her to get the fuck out, and he didn't give a damn how she took it. Bella's feelings had never mattered to him anyway. Monty shook his head and started his ride, but instead of going to a hotel like he'd planned, his cell rang and sent him somewhere else.

Chapter 2

Chance sat in a private booth at the steakhouse he had invested in only a few months earlier, and waited for his protege to arrive. Business had been good since the establishment opened and was steadily booming. It made Chance think seriously about going legit. He had lived a good and long successful life in the dope game, but he was ready to retire and put up the scales.

Chance was a different breed of dope man than those he encountered on a daily basis. He pushed hard and gave it all he had just so he could make it to the top of the food chain. He would always put the money he made into shit that would hold him down in the future. Things that wouldn't snatch his freedom or put a bullet in his dome. Chance had never really been into the flashy diamond-encrusted Jesus pieces or the gold-banded Rolex watches. He was fine with just a Cuban link and a simple black Casio watch. He also never cared about rocking designer fits like the next nigga, but still managed to stay fresh and looking like a million bucks.

Chance had called for Monty to meet him so he could break the news of his retirement. He also wanted to ask him to pull back from the streets and take over his throne instead, but before he could fully give Monty the reins, Chance had some real shit he needed to get off his chest. However, he knew Monty wasn't going to like what he had to say.

"Chance. My mufuckin' nigga. What it do, bruh?"

Chance stood at Monty's presence out of respect for the young G—respect he felt Monty had truly earned. Chance had done his best to pass along all the street knowledge he possessed because he wanted Monty to be as successful as he was. However, somewhere along the way, Monty lost focus of his priorities, and that was something that could cost him in the end. Chance wanted to save him and prevent the loss, but he knew that, at the end of the day, it would all be up to Monty to save himself.

"Montana. Glad you could make it on such short notice."

"Ah, come on. You know I'ma always show up when you call, no matter what I'm doing."

"That's real. Come on and sit down with me. I have some things that I need to discuss with you."

"What's up with you sounding all serious and shit? You got someone I need to handle for you? A mufucka better know they will lose their life for fuckin' with you. Just tell me who it is, and I got you."

"No, Montana, that's not the reason I asked you to meet me here, so chill out. I want you to know that the things I taught you were for your protection in the game, not for your pleasure, and you're starting to embarrass me."

Monty gave Chance a look as if he'd tried him, and in a way, he had. Monty had no clue what he was talking about. He couldn't think of anything he'd done to warrant Chance to feel the way he did, so he needed some type of clarification.

"The fuck you mean? Embarrass you? All my moves are precisely made by using the knowledge and skills you taught me. Shit didn't seem like an embarrassment then, so what makes now any different? I'm just out here being the man you made me."

"See, that's where you're wrong. For some reason, you ain't that man anymore, and what I want to know is why. I used to be proud when people compared you to me, 'cause it made me feel like I'd done something right, but here lately, I don't know how to feel. You out there doing some stupid shit, and damn it, I will not continue to stand for it."

"Yo, Chance, you trippin'. Why don't you stop hesitating and tell me what's up? 'Cause I don't know what the hell you talking about. Ain't shit changed about me but upping the cash flow. Ya boy bringin' in big faces like a mufucka, and the amount I push your way should say everything. So however the fuck you feel is wrong."

Chance had to take a deep breath in order not to lash out the hard way on Monty. He didn't know where the disrespect had come from, but it wasn't something he could take kindly to. If Monty didn't change up his tone after a warning, things between them would go sour quickly, and they would never be the same.

"First of all, you need to tone that shit down and check that attitude you got pressed on your shoulders. I've never shown you disrespect, and I'll be damned if I take any from you. Ya feel me?"

"Yeah, Chance, I feel you. That's my bad, and I do apologize. I'm just not liking what you coming at me with when I ain't done nothing wrong. I just need you to enlighten me a bit."

"Your apology is accepted as long as you can remember not to handle me like that again. Now, I needed to see you about a couple of things, but first things first, and you better listen to me carefully."

"I'm all ears, bruh. You have my complete, undivided attention."

"And for your sake, I better keep it. Anyway, you've been in them damn streets long enough to know that a turf war ain't where it's at, so don't start one, and don't play on my intelligence and tell me that my information is wrong, because my sources are pretty damn solid."

"Ain't nobody trying to start a turf war, but my area should be respected. If I find out some random mufucka is out there pushing dope on my block, his ass getting dealt with."

"Your block? When the fuck did it become yours? Last time I checked, that block belonged to the entire hood. You don't own them streets, Montana. They belong to the city, and the sooner you realize that, the better off you will be. There is plenty of food out there and you need to learn to share it before you end up being the one starving."

"Come on now, Chance. Cut me some slack. You know as well as I do that he had no right to just show up like that and start serving where me and my people serve. When the hell did it become okay for the opps to push where we push?"

"The opps? Just who are the opps, Monty? Come on and enlighten me. You can't. Can you?"

Chance waited for a moment just to see if Monty would respond, but somehow, he already knew that he wouldn't, so he continued.

"Oh, so you ain't got no answer for me, huh? I find that funny since you the one swearing the opps sent him out there. Ya know what? I'm a go head and do you a solid, though and tell you who he worked for. He worked for himself. He was out there for his girl and their newborn son. That lil' nigga was on a come up to feed them. He ain't never sold dope in his life, but since he was down on his luck and had an extra mouth to feed, he decided to cop a small package in hopes of doubling his funds so he could make ends meet."

"So why he ain't just say that instead of playing all hard like he worked for a major player?"

"He ain't owe you no explanation. Who the fuck are you for somebody to be checking in with? Tell me, when your life is on the line, you gone play pussy or you gone go out like a G? When mufuckas sign up for that street shit, they got to play it all the way through. Ain't no half steppin' in the game and you of all people know that"

"He still should have put me up on it. Things might have turned out different for him if he would have"

"Fuck what you saying because it would have turned out the same way regardless of what he would have told you. What you should be worried about is who gone feed his family now. Are you gone make sure they eat, or you gone keep moving and forget that they need to?"

"That's real low, Chance. You know I ain't even like that. I guess I deserve that, though."

"Yeah, Montana, you did deserve that and with that being said, I'm a need you to step up and do better."

"Aiight, I'm a do better. I give you my word."

"Well, your word better mean something because I'm about to pass you the reigns and I need to know that you can hold on to them without bringing drama to the set. You can't be doing dumb shit like that when you at the top. That's the quickest way to get knocked right back down."

Monty scrunched his brows and looked at Chance with confusion. He didn't quite understand what Chance meant, but if he had heard him correctly, Monty was about to move on up.

"Hold up. Did you just say what I think you said?"

"You heard me loud and clear. It's time for me to step down. I've been doing this a long time and now, I'm ready to sit back, relax and enjoy the fruits of my labor. I need someone to take over where I leave off. Someone I can depend on to handle the job right. I was kinda hoping that someone would be you. Should I question that, or are you ready to make that move?"

"You damn right I'm ready. That's what you groomed me for, and I must say that it has been an honor to serve under you, but to have the opportunity to be where you are, that means something. What's going to happen with you, though? Your black ass gone be bored with nothing to do."

Chance laughed at the comment, but he straightened it real quick.

"Monty, I've had my hands in the pot ever since I was a jit, but I never planned for it to be a life long career. Shit, I'm lucky I even still have a life. Sometimes, you got to know when its time to move on and that time has come for me. I earned my respect in the game and I gave that same respect to others. You must do the same. You have to keep peace, but you can't do that by being a greedy mufucka. All that turf bullshit you young niggas got going on, is just that. Bullshit. Let it ride and you will go a long way."

"Damn, Bruh. I don't even know what to say."

"All I need you to say is that you ready to start making big boy moves and the rest will fall in place."

"I am ready, Chance. I'm ready to step in to your shoes and continue your legacy. Who knows? Maybe one day I can pass along all that you taught me to another young up and comer."

"That sounds good, but before you do that, maybe you should go and visit your father. You might find that you have more to pass along that what you learned from me"

Monty nodded at the comment, because it was something he had already thought about. He had always been curious about his father, but had known better than to ask his mother.

Now that Monty was grown and could make his own decisions, he knew just what he had to do. He just didn't know when he would finally decide to do it.

"Maybe I will, Chance. Maybe I will."

Chapter 3

Monty cruised down the block, his eyes scanning the turf as his mind wandered over his newfound fortune. He had to be one lucky mufucka to have an entire drug empire handed over to him. The only thing he ever had to do to earn that spot was stay loyal and be patient. Monty was now the head nigga in charge, the connect, the plug, the mufucka everyone would have to see if they planned to continue pushing drugs through the hood.

Monty held the utmost respect for Chance and was grateful for the opportunity he had bestowed upon him. After all, it was Chance who taught him everything he knew about being gangsta. However, Monty was really nothing like him at all.

Monty liked being in the middle of the street action. In fact, that was what he lived for. He knew deep inside, it was gonna be hard to just sit back and wait on a mufucka to need a re-up. He enjoyed that fast-paced lifestyle, and not to forget, all the hood fame it brought him. Monty could care less about the fact that it could land him behind the razor wire or, even worse, in a closed casket. Monty liked to be seen. It made him feel important, plus it kept many bitches sweating his nut sack.

As Monty was about to turn a corner, he noticed his boy, Dreybo, leaning against his brand-new Tesla and decided to pull over and holla at him. Dreybo was a few years younger than Monty, but just as wise. They had bonded over how much they had in common. Dreybo was actually one of the few cats Monty felt like he could trust. The two of them had gone on a couple of capers together about six months prior, and to that day, no one else knew about it—not even Chance, and he usually knew about everything that went down in the hood. Monty fucked with Dreybo hard and couldn't wait to share his good news.

"Sup, my nigga? I see you still pushing that gas guzzler. When you gone grow up and get you one of these bad boys here? Shit, it'll save you plenty money. Means you'll have more to spend on some pussy."

Monty laughed at Dreybo's comment, but other than that, he paid it no mind. Dreybo thought he was a comedian and was always trying to crack jokes. He had been trying to get Monty to cop a Tesla for months, but it just wasn't his type of ride.

"Nah, bruh. I'm cool with what I got. Besides, you the only mufucka I know that still pays for pussy. That shit gets thrown at me."

"Oh yeah? That's what you say, but I still get the most pussy."

"Whatever, Drey. But you need to be careful with that, because while you think you the one fucking the pussy, it might actually be fucking you. Know what I'm saying?"

"What the ruck ever, Monty. At least I'll die a happy mufucka."

Dreybo held up his wine cooler as if he were making a toast, then turned the bottle up to finish off what was left. He'd never been able to handle the heavy stuff and often got teased about it. Dreybo had never been one to care about what others said, but he had to admit, the teasing sometimes fucked with his nerves. However, he would never let a mufucka know it.

"I see your soft ass still sipping on those girlie drinks. When you gone toughen up and get down a real man's brew? That shit is embarrassing. Matter of fact, I'm gonna make a deal with you. When you top off a bottle of gin, I'll go down to the lot and try out one of them rides. What do you say?"

"How about I just stop pressuring you to get one? Just don't get mad when your bitch wants to ride with me."

"Whatever, nigga. Speaking of bitches, though, whatever happened to that thick-ass red broad you was fucking with? I thought you two were solid."

"Man, I had to let that crazy bitch go. Besides, she was broke as a mufucka, and I'm tired of fucking broke bitches. What I need is a rich bitch. Rich in knowledge, rich in heart, rich in big faces, but most of all, I need her to be rich in pussy. Know what I'm saying?"

"Nigga, you shot the fuck out, but I know exactly what you saying. However, stick with me and a rich bitch will be the farthest from your mind."

"What the hell is you talking about, Monty?"

Monty smiled and walked closer to Dreybo, even though the two of them seemed to be the only ones around. Monty whispered just to be safe. Word about him would be out soon enough, but at that very moment, he only wanted his closest allies to hear of his promotion. Monty was already aware of the fact that he would have many haters, but he was ready for whatever they had to bring. However, he wasn't about to let them stop his flow.

"Chance pulled out and passed the keys to the whole city over to me. Every mufucka out here depends on me now, but you. Nigga, I want you at my right hand. You done had my back on so much shit, and because of that, I want to share the wealth and the status. Ain't no way I can do it without you. You've proven to me ten times over that I can trust you, and I can't say that about anybody else. Know what I'm saying? So, you wanna roll with me or what?"

"Hmm, you mean to tell me that Chance just up and turned over the reigns to you? Why the hell would he do that?"

"The fuck you mean, why? Nigga, I been loyal to Chance from day one. This is the position he groomed me for, and now, he truly believes I'm ready for it. What's up with you,

Drey? You supposed to be happy for me, but it seems to me that you hating instead. That ain't even like you."

"I ain't hating, Monty. You got it all wrong. You know that you my mufuckin' boy and I will always stand up and applaud you on all you succeed in. Shit, if anybody deserves that spot, it's you. I'm just shocked because I guess I always thought that Chance was in this for life. What's he gonna do now? Mufucka gonna be bored outta his mind."

"Nah, ya see, Chance already got shit held in place to keep him occupied. He got that restaurant thing going on and, from what he said, that place is moving up better than he expected. He's gonna be just fine."

"So that nigga gonna be a square now. Shit is just funny to me. Chance was a veteran in the game, and even though I hate to see him walk away from everything so soon, I commend him. Chance got courage to know when he's had enough, and I can't do nothing but respect that. Most mufuckas feel like it ain't gone never be enough, so they keep going until one day they got a gun pointed at they head or a metal door slamming in they face."

"Well, that ain't gone never be me. Mufuckas have to beat my alarm clock to catch me slipping."

"And since you put it like that, I would be honored to serve beside you."

"Then I guess we should go celebrate."

"Sounds like a plan to me."

The two of them got in their ride and drove to 'Cutters', a newly opened strip club that had been dominating all the rest ever since its first day of service, due to the explicit performances the dancers would put on. Going to Cutters was like watching live porn because nothing was off-limits. However, the city officials had already met up and filed the necessary paperwork to have it shut down. They cited that the content it advertised was disrespectful to the community, but the patrons who frequented the place thought differently.

So, Monty and Dreybo decided to enjoy the ultimate experience while they could.

"Shit, Monty. The bitches in this place is raw for real. Them city crackas need to chill out and come in here so they can see this for they self. Maybe then, they'll forget all about trying to shut the doors on it. What do you think?"

"Who knows? Maybe they will get the word and come see that these hos is top of the line, prime. Hell, anything is possible."

Just as Monty said it, a thick, dark-skinned sista with nothing on but a pair of six-inch heels and a belly chain approached them. Her wide, baby-making hips accentuated her flat stomach and coke bottle shape. Her nipples were fat and poked out like arrows about to hit their prey, and when Dreybo reached out and pulled on one, she smiled and introduced herself.

"Hey, sexy. They call me Cocoa, and for a small fee, you can find out why."

Dreybo lifted his brows. He was shocked at her bluntness, but he liked it. He had been to many strip clubs, but had never been propositioned in such a way. He looked Cocoa up and down and licked his lips. Dreybo had to admit that he liked what he saw, so spending a couple stacks on her would be well worth it. True enough, him and Monty had just gotten there, but he was ready to put in some work.

"Hey, bruh, I don't think I want to pass this blackberry up. You gonna be cool until I get back?"

"Go 'head, mane. I'ma get a table and just chill for a minute. Maybe take a couple of shots to the head and then find me something to snack on. Know what I'm saying?"

"I feel you on that tip, 'cause I'm 'bout to find out if it really tastes like Cocoa. I'll catch up with you in about an hour."

"An hour? Nigga, all this pussy in here waiting to be smashed and you gone spend a whole hour on just one?"

"Yeah, nigga, an hour. If the pussy good, I might be even longer. I'm the type that likes to take my time. You know, finesse the ho first. Make her feel extra special, like she the only bitch I see. Then, I pull out this monster and put it in her life. Makes getting that nut a little more meaningful. You should try that step sometime, so you can see just what I mean."

"Man, fuck that. I don't mind pulling out an expensive bottle of champagne and popping the top, but I ain't into all that romance and finessing shit. I'm just trying to fuck. But go head. I ain't gone knock you for doing ya thang. Just know that I'll be here somewhere getting my dick sucked when you finished."

"A'ight, Monty, do you while I go and find out just how chocolaty Cocoa really is."

Cocoa smiled and winked at Monty, then turned around and led the way as Dreybo followed closely behind her. Monty just shook his head and laughed at Cocoa's gesture and hoped that she turned out to be all Dreybo wished for. Monty hadn't expected his partner to jump in some pussy so quickly. He thought that they would go there, get some drinks, and chill while they watched some ass shaking and pussy popping before they chose someone to spend some time with. But Dreybo had changed up the whole game plan.

Monty took his time and looked around the club. He noticed that in the middle of all the horny men, there were some females in attendance. He liked a bitch who didn't mind watching another woman do their thang and decided that he would pick one of the lovely ladies from the audience along with one of the dancers and secure a room for the rest of the night. Fuck what Dreybo had planned, because Monty couldn't think of anything better than having two sets of lips on his dick at the same time. Then, he wanted to watch them do each other. His manhood hardened just from the thought of it, but suddenly, a voice disturbed his fantasy and brought him back to the here and now.

Her skin was the color of creamy peanut butter and looked like it felt just as smooth. She had on a baby-pink crop top that stopped just above her navel, which held a diamond piercing. The money-green boy shorts, which just happened to be Monty's favorite color, hugged her fat camel toe just right. The king cobra tattoo that wrapped around her left leg and all the way up to her thigh looked as if it was ready to take a bite and fill her full of venom. Monty could tell that she was just under five feet tall, but the six-inch red-bottomed heels she wore made her appear as if she could play for the WNBA. Monty was taken aback by her reddish-brown shoulder-length curls and her light hazel eyes. All of a sudden, everything else around him no longer seemed to exist.

"Good evening, handsome, and welcome to Cutters. My name is Cara, and I'm going to be your host for the night. Is there something I could get for you?"

For some reason, Cara seemed a little out of place to Monty. It also appeared as if she was uncomfortable, and it gave him an uneasy feeling. Cara just didn't fit in like the other females that worked there. However, Monty had never been one to go with his gut, especially where his dick was used to leading the way.

"Well, hello, Miss Cara. My name is Montana, but everyone close to me calls me Monty. And what you can get for me depends on if you're on the menu or not."

Cara giggled like a young girl, but Monty wasn't fooled. He could tell that she was all woman. Even a blind man could see that, and if he got his way, she would be lying up under him for the rest of the night.

"Uh, I'm flattered, but no, I am not on the menu, but here is a pamphlet with everything and everyone that is. Perhaps you'll find what you're looking for in there."

Cara handed Monty a three-page brochure with photos and short bios of different females. He quickly scanned through it and then handed it back to her. He had never really been turned on by something that came easily to him. Monty liked a challenge and the anticipation that led up to it. Besides, his mind had already been made up. Monty wanted Cara, and he would stop at nothing to have her.

"Nah, ain't none of this what I'm looking for. I want you, and you standing here playing hard to get, but thankfully for you, I ain't the type of nigga that gives up easily. How about you think on that while you show me where the important people sit at?"

Cara giggled and shook her head before she led Monty to the VIP section. All around him, hoes were shaking their bare asses for any man or woman who held up a few dollars in their hands. However, Monty was only focused on one thing: Cara's backside. He loved the way the bottom of her ass cheeks peeked out from the edges of the boy shorts and teased his manhood. Monty had already imagined himself in the middle of them, licking her ass crack from top to bottom until she came. His instincts made him reach out in hopes of copping a feel of her ass, but before his hand got close, she pushed it away and broke him from his fantasy.

"I wouldn't do that if I were you. I've already told you that I am off limits and I don't like to be violated."

"A'ight, that's my bad, but I can't help myself. I just don't understand how you working in a place like this but you ain't doing what the others do. What's the deal with that? 'Cause shit seems strange to me."

"Well, not that it's any of your business, but I only work here a few nights a week waiting tables to earn extra money. I have bills and a student loan to pay off. They have to get paid somehow, and I'm not the type of female that depends on a man to take care of me. You okay with that?"

"Damn, you straightened the hell outta me real quick, and I can't do nothing but respect that."

"Good. Now here is your table, and when your friend comes from the back, I'll show him where you're at. Anything else?"

Monty smiled at Cara and shrugged. Her feisty attitude was cute and turned him on even more. It was just what he needed in his life. He felt like Cara was wifey material, but he needed to figure out how to convince her of the same. Monty decided then and there that he wasn't going to fuck with any other females that night in hopes of gaining some favor from Cara. He had never been the type to cut his losses and move on because he felt like anything he wanted, he should have, and that included Cara.

Monty decided that he would sit down, order a few drinks, and chill for a little while. Then, he would try his luck again, but before he had a chance to relax in the plush VIP booth, everything went black.

Chapter 4

Monty opened his eyes to a bright light and a killer headache. At first, he thought his head was pounding from a hangover, but he couldn't remember drinking that much the night before. Actually, he couldn't remember drinking anything at all.

A beeping sound suddenly drew his attention, and it wasn't until then that he noticed an IV line stuck in his arm. Monty sat up, looked around, and then yanked it out. He had no clue why it was there in the first place, but he knew that somebody had better start explaining.

When Monty slung his legs over the side of the bed, a sharp pain pierced his insides. However, not one to be defeated, he pushed that feeling to the side and stood. But as soon as Monty's feet hit the ground, he began to topple over. Thankfully, before he could hit the tile face-first, he felt someone's arms around him.

"What are you doing, Mr. Hardy? It's really important that you stay in bed until you fully heal."

That voice—Monty knew it like a hook in a verse. He looked up, expecting a hallucination, but there she was. Cara. Same pouty lips, same long legs—but now wrapped in scrubs instead of those little bitty painted-on boy shorts from the club. She was just as sexy in them scrubs. Clean, sharp, professional—like someone who knew how to handle a bullet wound *and* a lap dance.

He blinked at her. "Hold up. You're a nurse?"

She smirked, pulling on a pair of gloves. "Two weeks away from finishing my ADN, actually. I am doing my final clinicals at County.

Monty shook his head, still staring. "Man, I thought you were just some random club girl. You got me feelin' like I misjudged the hell outta you."

"Well, maybe don't assume every woman in shorts is just there to dance for you."

"Now see, if you give a nigga a chance, he might actually sit his ass down."

"Well, it's good to know that you can find some humor in the midst of all that happened last night. But, Mr. Hardy, I'm going to need you to lie back down so I can re-dress your wound."

Cara pointed to Monty's right thigh, which caused him to look down. As soon as he saw the blood seeping through his hospital gown, he backed up and sat back down on the bed. Monty tried his best to recall what had happened to him, but for some reason, his mind drew a blank. He looked up at Cara and hoped that she would bring him up to date.

"The fuck did this happen? I mean, I remember you and being at the club, but I don't remember hearing any shots ring out."

As Cara lifted up the gown and changed his soiled bandage, she explained to him what had gone down the night before.

"First of all, you're lucky to be alive. Had that bullet gone a little more to the left, you and I wouldn't be talking right now."

"Bullet? You mean, I got shot?"

"Yeah, you did, along with several others, and thanks to you jumping up from your seat and blocking me, I'm still breathing and able to tell you about it."

"Oh shit. So that makes me your hero. That mean you gone give me a shot now?"

"Yep, Mr. Hardy, I am going to give you a shot, but I can assure you that it's not going to be the kind you're looking for. Now, if you could please turn over on your stomach and relax your muscles, I need to administer some antibiotics to ensure you don't get an infection."

"Hold up? Why I got to lie on my stomach? Where the hell you putting that long-ass needle at?"

"I'll give you one guess."

Monty already knew where she was going to give him the shot, but he wanted to hear her say it. For some reason, to hear it come from her lips made it less traumatizing. He had never been the type of man that liked anything around that area. Unless, of course, he was deep inside of a bitch and she had her hands on his ass cheeks, pushing him deeper. He could already envision that bitch being Cara. He just needed to make her feel the same way.

"A'ight, Miss Cara. I'm about to make a nice deal with you that you won't be able to turn down. First of all, you can stop with that Mr. Hardy bullshit, 'cause I feel like we have moved well beyond the formalities by now. You call me Monty and let me take you out once I'm released from here, and I'll let you put those pretty little hands of yours anywhere you want."

"Uh uh, no deal. I don't date men like you. I prefer the ones who do things the legal way. Therefore, I never have to worry about my livelihood being put in jeopardy."

"Now don't you think you should get to know me before you stereotype me? How you know I ain't doing legal shit?"

Cara reached over, opened a small side drawer, and pulled out a manila envelope. She raised her perfectly arched brows, then passed the envelope to Monty.

"This is how I know you ain't legit. Remember, I'm your nurse, and it was my job to undress you and gather your belongings before the cops did."

Monty opened the sealed envelope and looked inside, where he found several small baggies of crack cocaine and marijuana. Inside was also several knots of hundred-dollar bills and three blunts. He pursed his lips together before closing the envelope back up, then something else came to his mind.

"Wait a minute, you said there was shooting. My boy, where the hell is Dreybo at? I know he had to have made it out of there. Is he here in another room? I need to see him to make sure shit's sweet."

"No, Monty, I'm sorry, but if you're talking about the man you entered the club with, he didn't make it out."

"The fuck you mean, he didn't make it? I ain't trying to hear that shit. I'm a need you to take me to him now."

"Monty, Andre Tilley was found DOA in one of the back rooms along with one of the dancers. His injuries were too severe, and there was nothing anyone could do to save him."

Monty couldn't believe what he had heard, but somehow knew that it was the truth. He held his head down in the palms of his hands and wept for his fallen comrade. Whoever said thugs didn't cry was sadly mistaken because Monty shed a bucketful for Dreybo, his right-hand man. The one he wanted to be seated beside him when he rose to the top. Other than Chance, Dreybo was the only nigga he could count on. They had made plans to do some big things and make some major moves, but those plans had been destroyed. Monty sat there and began to wonder if the hit on the club was just a random act of violence or was it a targeted hit.

"Aye, I need to get the hell up out of here. This shit just ain't adding up."

Monty was about to stand up from the bed again, but Cara stood in front of him and stopped him. He looked down into her eyes and swore that he could see her concern. Monty's nose flared in anger as visions of revenge flowed through his thoughts. Revenge on who, he wasn't sure of yet, but he wasn't stopping until he found out. A mufucka was going to have to pay, but at that moment, Monty knew he was in no position to deliver up some karma.

"Monty, you need to relax and let your wound heal properly. There is nothing you can do to bring your friend back, so at least do what you need to do so you don't join him."

"Look, your concern for me is nice, but I can't stay held up in here. I can't handle shit I need to handle up in this mufucka. I need to get home and since you seem so worried about me and my getting better, you can care for me there."

"In case you don't realize it, I do have a job and you are not my only patient. I have bills that I am already struggling to pay, and catering to you and your needs is not going to help me get that done."

"Okay. What if I pay you three times what you're making here? That should be enough to handle all your bills and then some."

"What makes you think I want to take care of you twenty-four-seven for the next few weeks? Even for that amount of money?"

"I figured that since you need the money and I need to be taken care of, it was a genius idea. This shit here is hindering me from handling my business. Know what I'm saying? Of course, you do. Now, you can either agree and help the both of us out, or you can continue to work here for pennies. It's your choice, but either way, I'm outta this bitch."

Cara grew silent and thought about the deal Monty had proposed to her. She told him that she had a student loan and bills to pay and knew that he was only trying to look out. Cara decided to take Monty up on his offer because honestly, what else was she going to do?

"Okay. I'm going to go and talk to my supervisor to let him know that I will be doing home health care for the next few weeks, but I am not going to quit my job. It's what makes me independent, and you have to give me your word that you won't try any freaky stuff. Remember that this is only temporary. As soon as I see that you're free from catching any infections and you are healed enough to do things for yourself, I'm out of there. Deal?"

"Whatever you say, ma, but after spending a couple of weeks with me, you may not want to leave."

Cara rolled her eyes at Monty and then turned around and walked out. Less than fifteen minutes later, she walked back in pushing a wheelchair.

"Alright, let's get you dressed and out of here."

"I ain't riding out of here in that thing. I'm used to high-end wheels, not fucking wannabe scooters."

"Very funny, but you either ride in this, or you don't ride at all."

"Damn, you drive a hard bargain. Guess you ain't giving me much of a choice."

Cara helped Monty get dressed and then grabbed his chart. As she pushed him to the elevator, it felt as if all eyes were on her, which made her uncomfortable until she remembered what her father always told her, and that was to never worry about what the haters said or even thought. So, with that in mind, she pushed on. Once Cara made it to her car, Monty shook his head and held his hands up in protest. Cara knew that the rusty old Buick Skylark she drove wasn't impressive, but it was paid for, and that was all that really mattered.

"Uh uh. Hell nah. I'm not getting in that. Girl, I can't let a mufucka see me riding shotgun in something so old. You can't do no better?"

"Look. It's true that this car is old and I've had it for a minute, but it serves its purpose. Unlike you, I don't need fancy and expensive rides to make me feel like I'm some damn body. Now you can either ride away from here in this, or you can go catch a damn bus."

Monty shook his head as Cara stood to the side of him and pouted. He knew that her feelings were hurt, but someone so beautiful shouldn't have been riding around in something so ugly. Monty was a gangsta, and he knew that he would be the joke of the hood if someone saw him riding in the broke-down Buick. Just like himself, he felt like Cara needed something that complemented her, and he was just the man to make that happen.

"I'm sorry, a'ight, I ain't mean to hurt your feelings or anything. Why don't you let me help you out and get you something a little newer, something that complements that pretty ass face of yours? What do you say?"

"Thanks, but I'm not looking for any handouts. This is what it is. Like it or not."

"Damn, lil momma, why don't you stop playing all hard and shit and let a nigga do a little something for you?"

"Yeah, and then be obligated to pull my panties to the side so you can hit it one time? No, thank you. Now, are you getting in or what?"

"Guess your feisty ass ain't giving me much of a choice, but just so you know, you may be driving to my place in this piece of shit, but you ain't leaving there in it. I'm replacing this mufucka and ain't shit you can do about it."

"Boy, whatever."

Cara threw her hands up in defeat, then helped Monty get into the passenger side of her car. She shut the door after securing him in his seatbelt, then folded up the wheelchair and put it in the trunk. When she got in the Buick, she put the key in the ignition without acknowledging Monty. He liked her hard-to-get attitude and didn't mind working to gain her attention. Monty knew that he would just have to be patient, but he was dead set on wifing her. She was a breath of fresh air to him, and once she became his, he would cut off all other bitches he fucked with, completely.

Monty laughed and held his head down in embarrassment when Cara's car wouldn't start. He could tell that she was just as embarrassed as he was and almost rubbed it in. Monty was trying to gain her favor, though, not lose it. He didn't say one word as she continued to turn the key in the ignition.

Finally, it came to life, causing Cara to breathe a sigh of relief.

"Look, why don't you just go ahead and pull into the dealership on the way to my crib, because honestly, I don't think this thing right here is going to take us very far, and in case you don't remember, I'm in no position to be stranded on the side of the road."

Cara finally swallowed some of her pride and agreed. She knew that she needed a more dependable ride and decided she had better not pass one up.

"Okay, but I'm going to pay you back every single penny. So if you don't mind, I'd appreciate something that I can afford."

"Don't worry about all that. This ride is included in the deal for you taking time off from your job to take care of me. I mean, you doing home health care means you need to be pushing something dependable. Consider it paid for. No paybacks."

Cara knew there would be no reasoning, so she agreed to Monty's terms and drove off the lot in a brand new Benz.

"Thank you for this. I really do appreciate it, but you still ain't wetting my panties up."

"Don't worry. They say good things come to those who wait. And luckily for you, I'm a patient ass nigga."

Cara just shook her head and pushed on. She had to admit that she did like Monty's style. He was much different than she ever could have guessed. However, when it came to her, he was going to need a lot more than patience—he just didn't know it yet.

Chapter 5

Cara wasn't sure what to expect when she pulled up to Monty's mini mansion, but the sight that greeted her took her breath away. The place was everything she'd imagined and more. Monty had noticeably done very well for himself. The two-story structure stood like a fortress, its sleek modern exterior gleaming in the afternoon sun. The lush landscaping, with its manicured lawns and palm trees swaying in the breeze, only added to the aura of success. Monty's home was more than just a house; it was a statement.

But as much as Cara admired the grandeur, a knot tightened in her stomach. Monty had to know, deep down, that all of this—the house, the cars, the lavish lifestyle—was built on shaky ground. In the game, everything could be snatched away in a heartbeat, including his life. Nothing from the streets ever lasted. She'd seen it too many times before.

Still, what Monty did or didn't have wasn't her problem. She wasn't here to judge or get caught up in his world. But a small part of her hoped he could enjoy the fruits of his labor, at least for a little while, before the inevitable fall came. Life in the game was fleeting—something Monty would have to face sooner or later.

"So you just gone sit over there and admire ya boy's spot, or you gone help my broke-down ass get up them steps?"

Monty pointed to the steps that led to his front door and smiled. Cara looked to where his finger had led and raised her brows. There had to be at least thirty steps, and she wondered why, but dared not to ask.

"Sorry about that. I was just taking in the scenery, and I can see that you've done very well for yourself. I guess I just wasn't expecting all of this. I'm actually impressed."

"So what was you expecting? Some boarded-up, Section 8 corner house? I've worked hard every day since I was a jit, so I better have something to show for it."

Cara shook her head, then got out. She walked around to the other side of her brand-new car so she could help Monty get inside. She was glad that he had convinced her to leave the wheelchair behind with her Buick because there were way too many steps to try and master. She knew that her only option would be to put her arms around him while he slowly limped from step to step. She was almost certain that he wouldn't mind them being so close, so Cara draped an arm around his waist while he draped an arm around her shoulders. But before they made it halfway up, a voice stopped them in their tracks. Cara looked up and saw a cute Spanish female, and when she ran down the steps and leaped onto Monty, Cara let go.

"Oh no, Monty baby, what happened to you? Don't worry, Bella is here for you. Come, let me take care of you."

Monty pulled back from Bella because, even though Cara wasn't his woman yet, he didn't want her to get the wrong impression.

"Damn, Bella, I thought I told you to be gone by the time I came back. What the hell you still doing here?"

"No, Papi. You never tell me to leave. Besides, who will take care of you if I do?"

Monty looked at Cara, then back at Bella, and then answered her question.

"Not that I owe you an explanation or anything, but that's what she's here for."

"What? She knows nothing of taking care of you, and I will not leave you in her hands."

Before Monty could say another word, Cara decided to switch gears and speak up. The Spanish bitch was getting on her nerves, and from what Cara could tell, she was getting on Monty's, too.

"Look, Bella, or whoever the hell you are, Monty asked you to leave, and I think it is better for you to listen. He doesn't need you anymore because he has me now, so you can carry your ass back to Mexico or wherever it is that you come from, and please, do not make me tell you again."

Bella was speechless. She looked at Monty to speak up for her, but he didn't, and she could not believe it. So, Bella put her hands on her hips and gave Monty a piece of her mind.

"Fine, you want Bella to leave, I will, but do not ever contact me again. Mark my words, though, you will regret it, you bastard."

Bella turned and stormed back into Monty's house, and a few minutes later, came out with a bag and her cell phone in hand. She was about to ask Monty for a ride but thought better of it and called for a cab instead. Cara and Monty waited for the cab, and ten minutes later, Bella got in the back. She made sure to flip Monty off before the driver pulled away. Monty just shook his head at the childish act. He didn't have time for a bitch who had tantrums and was glad Bella was finally gone.

When the cab was out of sight, Cara helped Monty the rest of the way inside. When they stepped into the foyer, Cara could smell the last traces of Bella and told herself that she would clean that area as soon as possible.

"Should I be worried about any more of your women? Because that was a bit much, and I didn't agree to come here so I could be in the middle of your drama."

"Nah, there won't be any more surprises, so you don't have to worry. That one was my bad. Bitch was supposed to be gone before I came home."

"So, you have a habit of letting random women stay in your home while you're out looking for the next one, or was Bella just an exception?"

"Actually, Bella wasn't shit but a quick fuck, and she's the only one I've ever mistakenly had here more than two hours. The bitch got lucky because I got an emergency call and had to leave. Her still being here was only by default. Why you asking so many damn questions anyway? You feeling jealous or something?"

"Oh, I can assure you, it's not because I'm jealous. That bitch and any other one that wants you can have you. I just like to be aware of what's going on around me so I can be prepared, but since it seems as if I'm irritating you, I won't ask anything else. Now, let's get you to your room so you can get out of them jeans."

"I thought you'd never ask."

Cara could only shake her head at Monty because she knew that she couldn't admit that he was fine as hell. Cara also knew that spending time with him was going to make it very hard for her to walk away when the time came, and at that present moment, she wasn't sure how soon that would be.

Once Cara got Monty to his room, she sat him on the edge of his king-sized bed and helped him take his shoes and jeans off. She could tell that the pain in his leg was intense, although he tried to play it off as nothing. Once he was undressed, Cara could see the small amount of blood that had started to seep through the bandage.

"Damn, you're bleeding through again. I need you to lay back so I can change it again, and you're going to be bedridden for a few days. I know you don't like the sound of that, but if you don't stay off of it, that hole in your leg will never heal."

"Being in bed is not the part I mind. It's missing out on business I need to take care of."

"Uh, you don't have a partner or something to take up the slack? I mean, most dope boys have a so-called right hand."

"Yeah, in case you've forgotten, I have to bury mine."

"I'm sorry, I wasn't even thinking. Please forgive me."

"Ain't no biggie. It comes with the game. Guess I thought he would at least be able to play in it a little longer."

"That's what we all think, but when you indulge in the streets, there are consequences that come along with it. That's the main reason I don't date men like you. I enjoy waking up every day with no drama, no worries, and as far as I know, no enemies. You ever thought about getting out? Maybe doing something different with your life?"

"Hell nah. That thought ain't never crossed my mind."

"Well, I'm sure when you were younger, you had big dreams of being somebody successful. You know, maybe a doctor, a lawyer, a fireman. I mean, I've never heard of any boys saying they want to grow up and be a gangster or whatever it is you call yourself. You seem like you're smart enough to master something different."

"I could do whatever I want to do, but everybody knows that once you go gangsta, ain't no turning back. I tried that straight-A, good ole church boy shit, and it wasn't for me. This right here is what I was born to do. Ain't nothing else for me. I'm a ride till I die."

As soon as Monty said it, Cara yanked his old bandage off, causing him to wince in pain. She looked up at him apologetically, then continued. The whole time she cleaned and redressed his gunshot wound, she couldn't help but notice his dick. Cara could've sworn that it kept getting bigger with each touch of her hand, and as bad as she wanted to ignore it, she just couldn't.

"Uh, do you think you could do something with that thing? It's kinda distracting."

"I don't see what the problem is, but if it's bothering you so much, do something about it."

"Nice try, soldier, but that's not going to happen."

Cara finished with Monty's leg, then got up and walked out of the room, leaving him all alone. She told herself she wasn't staying there a minute longer. She had her boundaries—she wasn't some damn babysitter, and Monty was no one she should be getting attached to. He was dangerous, and the kind of man who could pull you into his world without even trying. But then, she remembered why she was there in the first place. She was getting paid well— very well. And no matter how attracted she was to him, no matter how much his charm made her blood run hot, she had a job to do. She couldn't afford to get caught up in Monty's world, but damn if he didn't make it hard to keep her distance.

Monty had told her that she could stay in any room she chose, but out of the four she had to pick from, she got the one that was closest to his. Not because she wanted to be that close—she just felt like she should be available should he need her. After all, he was paying her damn good, in more ways than he knew.

Chapter 6

Chance used the spare key and walked up in Monty's house like he owned it. He was pissed because he had been trying to reach him for days, and since it seemed like Monty didn't want to be disturbed, Chance decided to pay him a visit and find out why.

Chance heard about the shooting at the club by word of the streets . . . the same streets he called himself retiring from. He was curious as to why Monty didn't call and tell him about what had happened. Chance had attended the closed-casket memorial for Dreybo in hopes of finding Monty there, but for some reason, he was a no-show! Chance found that strange because he knew that Monty and Dreybo were thick as thieves.

When Chance walked into Monty's plush white and black living room, he heard a noise coming from the kitchen. He had never known Monty to do anything in the kitchen, so it immediately put him on high alert. Chance placed his hand on the butt of the nine millimeter he had stowed in the waist of his jeans and crept up. What he saw made him even more pissed than what he already was.

"So you up here playing house? The fuck you ain't answer my calls for? I been trying to reach your ass for days."

Monty and Cara both looked up from the plates of food they had in front of them as soon as they heard Chance speak. Monty put the fork he held in his hand down, pushed his chair back, then stood and limped over to where Chance was.

"That's my bad, but as you can see, I ain't been too good. But come on, Chance, respect my space."

"Your space would have been respected had you picked up the phone. You got shot in the leg, but ain't shit wrong with your mufuckin fingers. I had to hear about what happened from niggas around the block. I should have heard it from you, though. This bitch got you forgetting where your priorities lie? 'Cause if so, she needs to go."

Cara was appalled at the blatant disrespect Chance had shown her, but she wasn't about to intervene in what he and Monty had going on. Instead, she stood from her chair, and without saying a word, walked out of the kitchen. Not even a minute later, Monty heard his front door slam shut. He didn't try to stop her because he knew she would be back, but he would check Chance about her.

"Come on now, Chance. That shit wasn't called for. She's been here taking care of me so I can get better and get back on my grind. I don't need this to slow me down."

"Mufucka, you took a bullet to the leg, that's all. Don't let me find out that you been playing me all this time and you really pussy. I've had worse than that happen, and I still kept it moving. Besides, that ain't no excuse for not letting me know what was up. And why you wasn't at Drey's funeral? I thought your brotherhood with that nigga was solid."

Monty held his head down, not out of embarrassment, but out of mourning. He had tried to push thoughts of Drey's being dead out of his mind, but Chance had pulled it right back in.

"I couldn't do it, Chance. I couldn't stand there and see him laid out like that. Shit already fucking with me real hard. I had Cara send some flowers and my condolences, though, but I just couldn't will myself to go. I'm trying to remember my boy as he was, not as he is now. Know what I'm saying?"

"Nah, I don't know. You should have went and paid your respects. Much as you and him been through, don't you think he deserved that much? Shit ain't right, but hey, that's on you. Anyway, word is that the hit was targeted and the bullseye was on you. That should have been you in that casket, not ya boy. Didn't I tell you not to start a war? Especially one you ain't ready to fight?"

"So what you saying, bruh? You think that was a retaliation for that nigga I melted? I thought you said he was a nobody, just trying to make ends meet. Besides, nobody knows I had anything to do with that. I took out all the witnesses."

"Then how did I find out?"

"That's a good ass question, Chance. How did you find out? You got someone watching me or something? You playing two sides?"

"Okay, nigga, you can chill with all that. You need to be careful of the shit you say out your mouth. And you want to know who told me about it? Mufucka, you did. When I spoke to you about it, you ain't once deny it. You went right along with it. Don't you know that you should never admit to anything, no matter who it is asking you about it? Besides, the niggas that burnt up with him were from your set. It ain't hard for a mufucka to put it all together."

"Yeah, I guess you right, I'm just in my feelings right now about Drey, that's why I'm tripping. A mufucka gone have to see me about that, though."

"Oh, so you gone go out there with some payback, huh? Nigga, let that shit go."

"Let it go? You mean to tell me that you ain't never took out a mufucka on some revenge type shit?"

"I did, Montana, back when I first started out. But let me tell you the repercussions I dealt with behind it. I kill one of theirs, and then they kill one of mine. The cycle never ends. Do you know how many people I loved got murked because of that foolish ass bullshit?"

"Well, thankfully, ain't no love out there on my side. The only person I ever loved is gone, and it wasn't the streets that took her, so miss me with that shit you talking."

"I'm telling you, Monty, walk away and let karma do the rest."

"Yeah, that's easy for you to say. You ain't out there in it anymore."

"You right, I'm not, but when I learned what I'm trying to teach you, I kept my enemies closer than my friends. It took a lot to let shit be. I only wish I could have taken my own advice sooner, but hey, you can do what you want to do. You gangsta. I'm a just sit back and run my restaurant while you out there handling other shit. I've given you my advice, but the rest is up to you."

Right at that moment, Cara walked back into the kitchen carrying several shopping bags. She set the bags on the counter and then turned to Monty.

"I figured I'd step out and get a few groceries so you don't run out of food. How long you been standing on that leg?"

The question caused Monty to look down, and when he saw the blood on his shorts, he shook his head. He couldn't understand why it was taking his leg so long to heal. He felt like there should have been some kind of progress, but before he could speak on it, Chance had a few questions for Cara.

"Don't I know you from somewhere? You look real familiar."

Cara was thrown off by the question, but not answering it would make her look suspect.

"Well, you couldn't possibly know me personally, and as embarrassed as I am to say this, you may have seen me working the floor at *Cutters* from time to time."

"Nah, I don't hang in places that whores roam, but now that you mention it, I do find it kind of ironic that you worked at the same place my boy here got shot at. Look at you now though, you up in his shit, bringing in groceries like you wifey or something."

Cara stormed out of the kitchen once again because Chance was doing a little too much to fuck with her. Monty had seen the hurt in her eyes and decided that he should step up and defend her. He knew that Chance was leery of people he didn't know, especially women, because he had been snaked by a few of them. Chance felt like females always had a motive, but Cara was Monty's business, not his, and he didn't appreciate the way she had been treated.

"A'ight, Chance. Don't you think you being a little too harsh on the lady? She ain't did a damn thing wrong. Plus, she's the reason I'm alive. You don't know her or the predicament she's in. Besides, she's here with me, so you don't need to worry about her."

"You know what, Montana? You right, she is here with you, but I know a snake when I see one. Something ain't right with that bitch. I could see it in her eyes, but you ain't got to listen to me, playa. I'm a let you find out for yourself. Anyway, I had a meeting set up with you and my old supplier, but I'm not so sure it's a good idea."

"Come on, Chance, you know I ain't no dumb ass nigga when it comes to business. You passed the reins over to me because you knew I could handle it. Cara ain't no threat to any of that. As soon as my leg heals, she's outta here."

"You say that, but I've seen pussy take down all types of mufuckas."

"Well, guess what? She won't even give me the pussy. Now what?"

"Don't speak too soon, my boy. You know how to charm the hardest of them. Just be careful. I'll call you with the day and time, but Monty, make sure that bitch ain't with you."

Chance turned and walked out of the kitchen, and as soon as Monty heard the front door slam, he limped up the stairs to Cara's room. When he opened her door, he saw her lying on the bed sobbing and then went and sat beside her. He knew that her feelings were hurt, and honestly, he didn't know what to say to comfort her. Monty had never cared about others' feelings, but Cara touched a place deep inside of him and changed all that. When his mother died, his heart grew as cold as ice, and thanks to having Cara around, it was slowly warming up.

"A'ight, ma, don't let anything that comes out of Chance's mouth affect you. That nigga just sour, 'cause he done been did dirty by every female he ever fucked with. Now, he feels some type of way against all women. Once he sees that you only mean good for me, he will relax. Just give him some time."

Cara turned over so she could face Monty because to her, it sounded like he was talking forever with them. It was nice to hear and all, but being tied down with a man was not in her future plans.

"Look, Monty, I don't give a damn what others say out of their mouth, because my daddy told me to never let words determine my emotions. So my feelings were not hurt. I'm emotional from thinking about my father. And look, I know that you are hoping that something between us happens in the midst of everything, but I think we should keep things just the way they are. I'm also not ready to get my heart broken."

"What makes you think I'm a break your heart? And don't tell me it's because that's what dope boys do."

Monty lightly mushed Cara in the face and laughed. Then she punched him in the arm, which eventually led to the two of them play fighting. Cara had the best of Monty, until he flipped her over on her back. Then the two of them locked eyes. Once their lips met, everything that had happened before seemed to be forgotten. That was, until Cara felt something wet.

"Oh my God, we forgot to change your dressing. We need to get that taken care of."

"Can't it wait? I can think of something else I'd rather you be doing instead."

"No, it can't wait, but I can assure you, the sooner you get up and let me handle that, the sooner you'll be able to handle this."

Cara smiled and gave Monty the hope that he had been looking for. He had been ready to dip inside of her from that first night, but she wanted to play hardball. Finally, though, he would have her right where he wanted her. He just hoped that he could keep her there.

Chapter 7

Cara rode Monty's dick with purpose. She loved to see the faces he made when he was about to cum. She had even snapped a picture once on her phone just so he could see it for himself. He found it intriguing and decided to do the same to her. They would lay together, share a laugh at the pictures, and then make love all over again.

Monty held on tight to her hips as he met her thrust for thrust. He could see himself planting a seed inside of her, although it hadn't been something they discussed yet, but Monty felt like she would be down with it. He decided to wait a couple more months before he brought the subject up. In the meantime, he would let her stay on her birth control.

After Monty came, Cara slid up and down his pole a few more times and got hers too. Then she leaned down, kissed him, and then laid her head on his chest. Times like those were often, and they wished it never had to end, but business was business, and it had to be taken care of.

"Hey, you cool with taking a ride over to Brewster's and picking up that loot for me?"

"You know I got you, baby. I was actually thinking of going out and picking up some Chinese. All that good dick made me hungry. I can stop by that spot on my way back home."

"A'ight, bet. I got to go drop a few keys off to Darryl, but I shouldn't be gone too long. I'll get that done and meet your pretty ass back here."

Cara smiled and winked at her man. Ever since she and Monty shared that first kiss, they had kept things steady, and there was no turning back. Monty and Cara seemed to complement each other in everything they did, including the street game. At first, Monty had been against Cara having her hand in the street business he conducted on a daily basis, but she somehow talked him into it.

"Come on, Montana, you can't do everything by yourself. Just prep me on what to do and let me help you. Who else are you going to trust enough to sit at your right hand? From the way you talked, Dreybo was the only one you could depend on, but he's not here anymore to have your back. You don't have to do this alone, and I figured since you charmed yourself into my life and made me a very happy woman, it's the least I could do."

That was all that needed to be said for Monty to fall weak and give in to her. However, when he told Chance, it caused a rift between them. Chance still felt like Cara had a motive, and no matter how hard he tried, he just couldn't convince Monty of it.

"Montana, you need to take heed when I tell you that's not a good move. The fuck is you thinking? Come on, bruh. You only been with the bitch for a hot second. You don't know what she's capable of. I'm telling you, something ain't right with her. I can feel it. I passed the reins to you because I thought you had enough sense to handle it. Now you just gone pull in a bitch you just started fucking?"

"Come on, Chance. You tripping now, you ain't even in this no more, and with Drey gone, she's all I got to hold me down. Besides, she ain't showed me no snake side, and I really don't think she's going to."

"You know what? You ain't even trying to listen to me, so I'm gone go head and let you do you. But when the bitch gets you hemmed up, don't call me because I ain't want no parts of it."

"My bitch is legit. All I'm asking is that you don't judge her based on what those hoes you used to fuck with did to you. She ain't grimey like that."

"Ya know, Monty, if my black ass would have listened to my gut feelings back then, like I do now, them bitches never would have even been given the chance to do me dirty. Like I already said, you ain't got to listen to me, but don't let some pussy blind you and get you fucked up."

Of course, Monty refused to listen to the nonsense Chance had spoken. Cara was his ride-or-die bitch, and honestly, Monty felt like Chance was envious because he couldn't find one of his own. Monty vowed that when Chance realized that Cara was solid, he would tell him to kiss his ass and keep it moving. A mufucka wasn't going to talk shit about his woman and then think that everything was straight between them.

Monty pulled out of his driveway ten minutes after Cara did. He thought about all he had accomplished and had to admit that he was proud of himself. He had come so far from when he first started out. That hurt, confused, and misunderstood young boy was now a man. The boss of a drug empire that had been handed down by one of the best who had ever done it. Shit was going real sweet, and then Monty's phone rang and caused everything to go sour.

"Montana. Baby, they took everything I had. I'm so sorry. I tried to fight back, but I was no match. Please, baby, please come get me."

The sound of Cara's voice in distress made Monty sick to his stomach. He had vowed that if she gave him a chance, he would protect her at all costs. He gave her his word that she would be safe with him, but he had to eat those words because a mufucka broke through his barricade.

"The hell you mean, they took everything? The fuck is you at, Cara? Baby, talk to me."

"I'm in the bathroom stall at the Burger King down the road from Brewster's. He don't even know this happened because I had already left his house. They ran up on me two blocks later at the stoplight. Jumped right in the car, put the gun to my head, and then made me drive to an abandoned house. The only thing I could save was my phone. Please, Monty, don't make me relive it, just come get me."

Monty had just left Darryl's but decided to send him a text. He sent Brewster the same text and drove on to the Burger King Cara said she was at. Monty just couldn't believe that someone had the audacity to run up on his bitch. They couldn't possibly have known that Cara belonged to him, because anyone who knew also knew not to try her in any type of way.

Monty knew that Cara's biggest fear was being involved in some drama because of who she dated. She knew the consequences of what came with dating a drug dealer, but because of Monty's promises, she gave in and gave him a chance. Now Monty hoped that what happened didn't cause her to have second thoughts about her future with him. Monty told himself that before he lost her, he would pull back from the game first, and he truly meant it.

Not even two minutes after Monty pulled into the parking lot, Darryl and Brewster pulled in behind him. As soon as he killed the engine on his ride and stepped out, Cara ran out of the restaurant and right into his arms. He looked at her face and could see her right eye already swelling and turning black. The one-inch slash on her cheek would leave a nasty scar, but in no way would it take from her beauty. A mufucka would have to pay for the violation. The streets would bleed until Monty found the culprit. Niggas would learn not to fuck with him or anyone that meant something to him.

Monty draped his tattoo-covered arm over Cara's shoulders and walked her to the passenger side of Darryl's F150 truck. She gave him a confused look because she just couldn't understand why she had to get in someone else's ride and not his. However, Cara respected Monty's mind enough not to ask questions. She felt like whatever choices he made on her behalf were for her own good.

Monty bent down and gently kissed Cara on the forehead and then shut the car door. It was only with her that he showed his softer side. Everyone else got the worst parts of him, and that would never change.

Monty knew that Darryl would keep Cara safe, so he had no worries sending her with him. Darryl had proven himself time and time again that he was loyal and could be trusted. He was also well aware of the consequences that came with betraying Monty or anyone he cared about, so he never thought of crossing that line.

After Monty gave Darryl instructions on what to do, the two of them gave each other dap and a brotherly hug.

"A'ight D, I'm gone need you to drive my girl home while I go somewhere and have a one-on-one with Brewster. I know you'll make sure she gets in safely."

"Now, boss man, you know you ain't got no worries when it comes to me. I got you."

Monty nodded at Darryl in agreement and then waited for him to drive off before he approached Brewster. He had put Brewster on his team because the young cat showed grown-man potential, and in the two years he had been on the crew, he never gave Monty a reason to doubt or worry. Monty wasn't so sure anymore, though, because what had happened to Cara shouldn't have happened at all.

"Come on and take a ride with me so we can try and figure out what happened and who was behind it."

"Nah, bruh. I'm cool talking about it right here. The fuck we got to ride somewhere for?"

"Mufucka, do you know who the hell you talking to? My girl got jacked after leaving your shit. Ain't nobody but you and me knew she was going there to pick up that gwop. Somebody said something and it wasn't me, so that leaves you."

Brewster threw his hands up and took one step back. The accusations Monty made were serious because Brewster knew it could cost him his life. He wasn't ready to die, and he knew that he had to somehow convince Monty that he was really telling the truth. Monty had put him on, and because of that, Brewster would never betray him.

"Look, boss, I don't know what you implying, but I ain't never been a disloyal ass nigga. Shit, you're the only one ever gave me a chance out here. You been nothing but good to me ever since that first day you put me on. I don't know about anyone else, but my momma always told me to never bite the hand that feeds me. You have to look somewhere else for your answers, bruh, 'cause I don't got none for you. Know what I'm saying?"

Brewster had never given Monty cause not to believe him, but Monty didn't know where else to look for someone to blame. He just couldn't figure out how anyone else could have known about the pick-up, and as bad as he wanted to put it on Brewster, he just couldn't.

"You say you ain't have shit to do with it, and for some damn reason, I believe what you talking, but if I find out anything different, you already know what's gone happen. Right?"

"I ain't worried 'bout that because you ain't gone hear no different. One thing I'm not is a pussy ass, scary ass nigga, and anything I do, I can stomp my name on it without fear. I ain't never went against you and never will, especially over some bread. I'm on your side, Monty, and ain't never had thoughts of crossing over."

Monty nodded and took in all that Brewster had said, and even though he knew it was true, he felt like he had to blame somebody. Monty knew from the jump that putting Cara out there like that was a bad idea, but he went against his better judgment because all he wanted was to make her happy, and he didn't care how anyone else felt about it.

"A'ight, Brewster, I'm gone head and take your word for it, but I'm telling you now that if I find out you had your hands in it, I'm cutting them bitches off, and I think you know by now that I mean everything I say. I don't make threats, only promises, and I keep them."

"I hear you, Monty, but these hands are clean. I'm gone talk to some people though, and see if I can find something out for you."

"You do that and let me know as soon as you hear anything."

Brewster nodded and turned around. He walked to his car with no worries and got in. There weren't many niggas he turned his back to, but he didn't like that him and Monty had any beef, even though Monty had questioned him about the move made on Cara. Everyone that knew Brewster also knew that his word was bond, and no matter who tested it, he would always pass.

Monty waited until Brewster drove away and was completely out of sight before he pulled out his cell phone. He felt like he needed to put a call into Chance so they could have a sit-down. Mainly, because Monty knew Chance had salty feelings toward Cara. He didn't really think that his one-time mentor would move like that, but he also didn't put anything past anybody. So, as soon as Chance answered, Monty went in.

"Sup, Chance? Yo sending mufuckas to pull jack moves how? Or nah, did yo do that shit yourself?"

"The fuck you think you talking to? Look, Montana, I don't know what the hell you been smoking, but you need to put that shit down, 'cause it's obviously got you tripping."

"I ain't been smoking on a damn thing. Somebody made a move on my girl, and they need to answer for it. Far as I know, you the only one got an issue with her."

"Man, fuck you and fuck that bitch. You wanna see me? You know where to find me. I'll be here waiting."

Before Monty could respond, a dial tone cut him off. He then jumped in his ride so he could go pay Chance a visit. Deep down in his gut, he knew that Chance didn't move like that, but because of the way he felt about Cara, he became the number one suspect. Monty had never been a pussy-ass nigga, so he knew he had to show up and show out. He felt that if he backed down, it would mean defeat. Monty had to let Chance know that if he had beef with his bitch, then he had beef with him too.

Monty pulled into the parking lot of the restaurant and got out. Chance stood outside and waited on him. He already knew Monty would show up, because it was what he would have done too.

"You said fuck me and my bitch? Well, here I go, mufucka. What's up?"

Chance stood with his arms crossed and looked at Monty as if he had lost his mind. He wasn't used to mufuckas trying him like that, especially one he practically raised. But if Monty wanted it, he could damn sure get it.

"What's up? Why don't you tell me, Montana? If I remember correctly, you the one that called me with that bullshit, and then you wanna rush over here like you gone get some straightening. As for me, I don't even know what the hell you talking about. You wanna explain?"

"I'm talking about my girl being jacked on her way back from a pickup. You the only one I know that seems to have a fucking problem with her being around. I just don't understand why, though, because she ain't never did a damn thing to you."

"Mufucka, have you completely lost your damn mind? Do I look like I need to pull jack moves on somebody's bitch? How dare you come to me and accuse me of some shit like that. I told you when you came up with the bright idea of pulling her in as your right hand, not to do it, but you did it anyway. Shouldn't have been too much of a loss though, since you only been pulling in pennies."

"Pennies? Oh, I see now, you an envious little bitch. I'm out here making moves you only dreamed of. Moves you ain't gone never make. I think that's why you passed over the reins. You was afraid of being embarrassed by having me in twitch you and surpassing everything you ever did. Just so you know, I would have done that anyway, because I was born with this shit in my blood. Even without your knowledge, I would have soared to the top and took over anyway."

"Hmmm, you know, Montana? You a funny mufucka. So damn funny, I forgot to laugh. I'm a tell you this, though. You came to me with some raw beef, but I'd advise you not to cook it up. This here ain't what you want, son. But if you choose to proceed, I'm a light your ass up, you understand?"

Chance then turned around and walked back inside his restaurant. He wasn't going to waste his time entertaining Monty's bullshit. He had more important shit to do, like call the plug and get Monty cut completely off.

Meanwhile, Monty thought about his next move. He knew that he had fucked things up with Chance and wasn't sure he was prepared to face the repercussions. He couldn't lie, Chance had been good to him and helped him get to where he was. Now, Monty was on his own, but he had an idea. He just hoped it went as planned.

Chapter 8

Cara had fucked Monty so good, it put him in a deep slumber, but the ringing of his cell phone disturbed his peace. He needed the rest because ever since his fallout with Chance, Monty had been on edge. The connect had cut off his supply, and the kilos he had stashed away were slowly depleting. There were other dealers he could buy from, but they were low grade compared to what he was used to. Plus, Monty didn't want to admit that his short rise to the top had fallen. He went from being the man to being just another dealer living day to day. True enough, he still had a few stash houses that his crew ran, but it was on the same level as everyone else.

Monty had seriously considered calling Chance and trying to make things right between them, but his pride kept him from doing so. He hated to admit that he was wrong, especially to someone of Chance's status.

Monty's phone continued to ring. He finally reached over and hit *ignore*. He honestly didn't give a fuck who it was. He couldn't think of anyone who would be calling him at that time of night anyway; however, it seemed like they had no plans of giving up.

Monty sat up on the bed and threw the covers off his naked body. He looked beside him and then around the room for Cara, but she was nowhere to be seen. He wasn't worried though, because Monty trusted her to the fullest.

After Monty planted his feet on the carpeted floor, he reached over and picked up his cell. When he answered, the words that came from the other side almost knocked the breath out of him.

"Yo, Monty, we been hit. Mufuckas came in while me and Chap were on a run. Everything's gone. What you want me to do?"

"What you mean? Come on, Gunzo, I don't need to hear that kind of shit right now . . . Fuck. How much we lose?"

"There was about fifteen left and a few that had already been broken down."

"What about the gwop?"

"About one twenty plus. All we got left is what we just put in our pockets, and ain't nobody talking. At least, not yet."

"A'ight. Take what you have on you and drop it to Poncho and Ski. Then take your ass out there and find my shit, or at least, who took it."

Monty didn't even give Gunzo a chance to respond before he hung up. Wasn't a damn thing Gunzo could have said to change shit, so he didn't want to hear it. After Cara got jacked for his loot and Chance had him cut off from the plug, Monty didn't think he could handle anything else. He felt like he was still too young and too fresh in the game to be going through so much. Shit just seemed to start going downhill for him ever since he got shot. Before that night, Monty had it all together—or at least that's what he thought.

Monty held his head in the palms of his hands, trying to figure out what his next move would be. He had been so lost without Dreybo and would give anything to have him back. However, that was not the way things worked, so he had to try and make the best of his bad situation.

"Baby, you okay? You need me to beat somebody's ass for you? Just tell me who it is, and consider it done."

Monty couldn't help but laugh. No matter what seemed to be going on in his life, Cara made it all worth it. She was his rock and knew how to brighten his day, every day. If all he ever had to do was spend time with her, he would be alright. When Cara sat on the bed beside him, he told her what had happened.

"One of my houses got jacked earlier. Gunzo and Chap were on a run when it happened. Gunzo said they took everything."

"I'm sorry, Monty. I know that it seems like when it rains, it pours, but you got to pick up that umbrella and keep it moving. You can't let things like that hold you back."

"Oh yeah? Well, if my shit keeps getting snatched, I ain't gone have nothing to move forward with. I got to find a new connect before I lose everything."

Cara was determined to take Monty's mind off of his misfortune, so she stood from the bed and dropped the silk robe she had on to the floor. She then pushed Monty back on the bed and straddled him like he was the seat of a Harley Davidson. She planned to start his engine and ride him all the way to paradise. Without any more words being said, Cara brought them both to an orgasm. But when it was all over, she took Monty back to a place he thought he had left behind.

"Some man called for you. Said he was your uncle and he needed to see you. Sounded kind of urgent."

Monty gave Cara a bewildered look because he knew exactly who she was talking about. It had been years since he'd heard any mention of his uncle Taboo. To be honest, Monty never even thought about him. Ever since Taboo told Monty that he was on his own, Monty moved the fuck on. He didn't even think his uncle was still breathing and wondered why, after all the time that had passed, he wanted to see him. Monty figured that Taboo wanted money or drugs; either way, he was shit out of luck.

"Far as I know, I only got one uncle, and I ain't never give him my number. Had no reason to. Mufucka took guardianship over me when my momma died, but only because the state promised him a check every single month.

Nigga ain't never gave a fuck about me, so I can't even begin to imagine what he wants to see me for."

"I don't know. Maybe he's had a change of heart. I mean, you are probably the only family he has. Just give him a call and see. I programmed his number into your phone."

"Yeah, a'ight, but that shit gone have to wait till the morning. I can assure you though, he ain't had no change of heart, 'cause his black ass don't have one. Come on now, who the hell puts a fifteen-year-old kid out in the streets to fend for himself?"

"People do change, Monty. You have to believe that."

"Yeah, but you got to wonder if it's for better or worse. I got enough shit on my plate already, and I'm still trying to digest what I've already eaten. I'm not sure that I can handle anything else."

"Well, that's what I'm here for. Whatever you can't carry, just pass it to me, and I'll carry it for you."

"Now see, that's why you my bitch."

The two of them shared a kiss and then fell asleep in each other's arms. And before they knew it, morning had shown up. Monty got up before Cara and got in the shower. He usually waited for her so they could take one together, but he decided to take one by himself so he could clear his mind and get ready for what the day held. He knew he had to get up with Taboo and see what the deal was, although it wasn't really what he wanted to do. Even though Cara had programmed Taboo's number into his phone, Monty would go see him instead.

When Monty pulled up to the small white stucco house, it made him think about his mother. Not because she had ever spent any time there, but because if she would have only lived, Monty would have never graced the house's door. And although he had only stayed in it for a minute, he deplored it just the same. He was actually grateful that Taboo had kept him from going in the state's foster care system, but other than that, Monty held no type of emotion for him. He had done Monty a solid by signing as his guardian, and because of that, Monty felt like he should show some kind of respect. That was the one and only reason Monty had pulled up in his uncle's driveway.

Monty shut off the engine of his ride and pulled his keys from the ignition. He then reached in the middle console and pulled out his nine, mostly out of habit, but also because he didn't know what to expect when he came face to face with the man who had signed up to be over him. Shit, somebody was out to get him, and until he found out exactly who it was, everybody was a suspect.

Monty's uncle Taboo stepped out onto the front porch of his house as soon as Monty stepped out of his ride. For a moment that should have been bittersweet, it turned out to be uncomfortable instead—especially for Monty—but he pressed on.

"You called and said you needed to talk to me. How the hell you get my number?"

"Now is that any way to talk to your uncle? Don't forget, I'm the one that saved you from a life of being bumped from one foster home to the next. So I don't think showing me some respect would be too much to ask."

"You still ain't answer my question. How did you know my number?"

"Hmm, well, whether you know it or not, my name, along with your father's, means something. That also means anything I want or need, along with him, of course, we get."

"Yeah, what the hell ever. Just tell me why you called so I can take my ass on. I got more important shit to do than to waste time here."

"Okay then, I'll tell you why I called. Your father, Montel, called me and asked me to tell you to go and see him. Said it's imperative to your future."

"Man, fuck him. His ass don't need to worry about my future. He ain't never gave a damn before. Why start now?"

"Montana, you got it all twisted up, son. Your father has always cared about you and what happens to you, and I know you ain't gone believe this, but I do too. I'll admit that when they called me and asked me to take you in, I was hesitant and really bitter about it. Your momma did everything she could to keep me and your father out of your life. I know it wasn't your fault, and I apologize for holding it against you and doing you the way I did. I do regret my actions because at the end of the day, it was her I was angry at and not you. I know she was only doing what she thought was best. I just hope that you will forgive me."

"Oh, so an apology is supposed to suffice for you putting me out there to find my own way in the streets just so I could eat? I was a fucking fifteen-year-old boy, and I didn't know shit about being in those trenches."

"But look at you now. The man to see. You wasn't on your own, though. I mean, you think Chance took you in by sheer luck? Nah, me and Montel put him onto you. That's your older brother. Got a different momma though. Came from a quickie Montel had in the bathroom at school when he was only sixteen. It was also his first time, and he didn't know that he was supposed to pull out. He don't regret it at all either. Chance is a good seed. It was too bad his momma didn't make it. Died right there, while pushing him out. Guess it was too much for her young body to take. He met your momma a year later, but she refused to raise him, so I had to raise him. I didn't do it for long though, because as soon as he figured out them streets, he was in 'em, and the rest is history."

Monty stood and stared at his uncle in disbelief. He wondered why Chance never told him that they were brothers. The thought burned Monty all the way to his soul. However, it explained why Chance took to him so easily. They were family, and somehow, Monty had managed to build a long bridge between them. The question was, who would be the first to cross it and make amends?

"You ain't got to forgive me, Montana, but at least forgive your father. I don't know all that your momma told you, but he did what he had to do. My brother, Montel, gave up the rest of his life just so you could live yours. Ain't no other way to put it. So please, go and pay him a visit. You at least owe him that much."

Without saying anything, Monty left, got in his ride, and drove off with a lot on his mind. The shit he heard was just too much for him to handle at that moment. Monty didn't want to believe that his mother not only fed him lies, but also kept the fact that he had a brother from him. He had always looked at her as a saint. She was the perfect being, an angel in his eyes, but his judgment had been clouded. He understood that she wanted to protect him, but he felt like he deserved the truth.

Monty slowly pulled into his circular driveway and parked. He noticed Cara sitting on the steps that led to his front door and wondered just how long she had sat there and waited for him. Out of all that could go wrong in his life, she was the one good thing that made it all worth it and all seem so simple. Monty couldn't help but wonder, though, if Taboo had already called and told her what happened, and as much as he trusted her, he was anxious to find out.

Once Monty stepped out of his ride, Cara met him halfway, but when she tried to wrap her arms around him, he pushed her away and lashed out.

"When the fuck did you and my uncle become such good friends? Huh? I'm just trying to figure out why he's so comfortable calling you."

"Monty, what in the hell are you talking about?"

"Look at you. Out here trying to comfort a mufucka like you in on what's going on. I guess he called and told you what happened, so now, you out here trying to comfort a mufucka, but I don't need that sympathy shit right now."

"Actually, Monty, he did call me, but only out of concern for you. I know that you going over there was hard, but I'm not the enemy, so don't make me one."

"You ain't the enemy? You sure about that? Because I'm starting to wonder."

"Fuck you, Monty. I don't need this shit."

Monty quickly regretted what he had said. He knew that Cara only had his best interest at heart. He had been wrong to be so tough on her and hoped she would forgive him, because the last thing he wanted was to lose her when he had fought so hard to keep her.

"Baby, look, I'm sorry. I know I'm tripping and shit, but so much been happening so fast, and it's got my fucking head spinning and my heart aching. You gone forgive a nigga or what?"

Cara looked Monty in the eyes to make sure that he was being sincere with his apology, and because she knew she couldn't stay mad at him for long, she smiled.

"Forgiving you is an option, but only under one condition."

"Oh yeah? Well, what's that? Go ahead and give it to me raw and uncut."

"You got to eat this pussy like it's our last time together."

"Damn, you a nasty bitch. Thankfully, for you, that's just how I like 'em."

Cara giggled and turned around. She led Monty up the front steps and then through the front door, but instead of leading him upstairs to their bedroom, she sat down on the fifth stair and laid back. Monty smiled and raised his eyebrows when Cara pulled up her nightgown and spread her legs. She snickered and then made the "come here" motion with her finger, and of course, Monty made it his business to dive in.

After Monty gave Cara what she wanted and put her to sleep, he decided that he should go and make things right with Chance. He wasn't too sure how it would go, but he had to make some kind of effort. After all, they were family. So after Monty got dressed, he went on his mission. He just hoped it wasn't a waste of time.

Chance was easy to find because he lived in a plush two-bedroom apartment that was located on the top floor of his restaurant. Monty had thought that after so much success in the dope game, Chance would have opted for a mini mansion to retire in—somewhere way out in the mountains, away from all the chaos the hood held—but he had been wrong. Chance liked to keep things simple, and no amount of money would ever change that.

Monty parked his ride in one of the reserved parking spots in the back of the restaurant, while Chance's ride filled the other. Chance had purposely gotten two reserved spots made—one for himself and one for whomever his future wifey would be. When Monty got out of his ride, he looked up. For some strange reason, he was nervous, but he knew it was something he had to do. He noticed that Chance's lights were still on and breathed a sigh of relief. Monty had to admit that he was on edge about the whole thing, but he had to pull through.

He walked around to the side door of the establishment because that was where the stairs were located that led to Chance's abode. But before he could push the buzzer to let him know he was out there, the door opened. The two of them locked eyes, and Monty felt like it should be him that broke the ice.

"Sup, Chance. I know I'm probably the last person you want to see, but could you give me a minute?"

Chance didn't respond but instead, opened the door farther so Monty could step inside. When Chance shut the door back, that was when he finally had something to say.

"You lucky that Unc called me, because the last time I gave you a minute, you brought me bullshit. Your ass better hope that ain't the case this time too."

"Yeah, about last time. I'm sorry about that. I was tripping for real, and I guess since you're the closest thing to me, I took shit out on you."

"Well, don't let it happen again, because if it does, I may not be so understanding."

"I'm cool with that, because I was dead-ass wrong and I won't ever try you like that again. I do need to know though, when was you gone tell me we were brothers? Didn't you think that was something I should have known?"

"Didn't think it really mattered much since we were so close, but yeah, we got the same father, and even if we didn't, I still would've looked at you as my brother. Me and you clicked from the very start. That was all that mattered to me. Plus, pops thought you may have felt some type of way."

"Hmm. I probably would have, 'cause you know my ass is petty, but I'm cool now. Shit, if it wouldn't have been for you, I wouldn't be who I am now. I'd also probably be in a jail cell or somewhere dead. You got me through a pretty rough time, and look at me. I repaid you by accusing you of some shit I know you really ain't do. That's my bad, bruh."

"It's all good. That shit is over with. Let's move on."

"A'ight, but I do need you to help me find out who pulled that move on my girl. Ain't no way I can just let that shit go."

Chance hesitated in his response because, honestly, he didn't give a damn who it was. He held no respect for Monty's bitch, but because he had respect for Monty, he knew that he had to step up.

"I can put some ears out there for you, but I'm telling you again, that bitch ain't right. I know you pussy-whipped and blinded by love so you can't see it, but your girl is a snake. I hope you figure that out before it's too late."

"I ain't come here to listen to you put Cara down. I know from day one that you've had some ill feelings towards her, and until her or I—either one—can change them, they are what they are, but I do ask that you stop dissing her around me. My bitch is legit. You understand what I'm saying?"

"Okay, I ain't saying nothing else. Just don't bring her ass anywhere that I'm at, and we'll be cool."

"I respect that, but I do have one more issue. I don't have a lot of product left, so I need you to turn the connect back on. I don't have nobody else."

"Nah, I can't do that. What's done is done. If you would've listened to me and kept ya girl out of it, you would still have plenty. Maybe you should go and pay our father a visit. He may be able to help you."

"Pops? What the fuck he got to do with anything? And how the hell is he going to help me from behind prison walls?"

"Just go and see him, and you'll understand why. Now, if we finished, my ass is tired, and I gotta get up early to meet with some investors about another joint. Maybe a nightclub or something. I don't know yet. Make sure you holla at me after you talk to pops."

"For sho. Have a good night, bruh."

Monty left satisfied with the outcome, even though he couldn't get a re-up on dope. He went home and hoped that something else would come through.

When he crawled back in bed beside Cara, he tried to fall asleep, but it eluded him. He thought about what Chance had said about going to visit their father in prison. When Monty was young, he had so many questions, but he knew better than to ask his mother. He knew that she would only get frustrated and tell him bad things. Now that Monty was grown, he still had those same questions and knew that there was only one way to get them answered.

Monty felt Cara suddenly stir beside him and looked over. He smiled at her and stretched his arm out so she could move closer. As soon as he wrapped his arm around her, she spoke in that voice Monty loved to hear.

"How did things go with Chance?"

"Hmm. I guess you could say it went the way it was supposed to. At least shit between us is right again."

"That's good to hear. Now maybe he will set things right for you with the big man so you can stop worrying so much about where it's going to come from. Maybe now you can set your mind to rest."

"Nah, I don't think that's going to happen, but it's all good. I'll find another source. Probably worked out like this for the best anyway."

"Well, at least now you two are cool again and hopefully be a family for real."

"Huh. Speaking of family, both Chance and my uncle suggested that I should go see my father in prison, but I don't know about that."

"You don't ever talk about him much, Monty, but maybe that is something you should consider. You never know, it could turn out to be a good thing."

"I don't know, Cara. Nigga ain't never been in my life. Just feels kinda strange to bring him into it now. I mean, what fucking purpose will that serve?"

"You'll never know unless you go and find out for yourself. Go and see what happens. I mean, what would it hurt? And if you're not feeling it, you'll never have to go again. I'll even go with you if you want."

Monty thought about what Cara had said and finally decided that one visit couldn't hurt. He just hoped his father didn't expect too much, too soon, because Monty didn't know how much of himself he could give, if any at all.

"A'ight, I'ma book the visit, but if I ain't feeling his vibe, I'm leaving and never going back."

"That seems like a fair deal, and at least you're making an effort and giving him that much."

"Yeah, I just hope that *much* is even worth it."

Chapter 9

Monty pulled into the federal correctional facility that had housed his father for many years. Monty had never been locked up himself, so he didn't know what to expect. However, he was almost certain that loneliness and despair were felt deeply on the inside. He couldn't even begin to imagine being one of the men who actually called the place home. He thought about the women and children the men had left behind and sympathized with them, because it was a hurt he knew all too well.

"I don't think I'm gonna be able to do this. I ain't ready. At least not yet."

Monty was about to start his ride back up, but Cara reached over and put her hand on his to stop him.

"Yes, baby, you can do this. You need to do this, and I'm going to be right there beside you every step of the way. Come on, Monty, you've come this far. You can't turn back now."

Monty thought about what she said for a moment and pulled his keys out of the ignition. Cara was right. It was something he needed to do. If for no other reason, for his sanity. He always told himself that he would go and visit his father one day, and now that the day had finally come, he knew he had to go through with it, or he would regret it for the rest of his life.

"A'ight, I'm gonna go in there and see what's up, but if I don't like how his ass is talking, I'm walking the fuck out. Nigga ain't been in my life for a long time, and if he wants to be in it now, he better have a damn good reason."

71

Monty didn't even wait for Cara to respond, and he knew that she understood why. She was cool like that, and it made his love for her even more real. The ho's Monty had been used to fucking with would nag him and never let shit go. Cara was a different breed, though, and Monty appreciated that. So, when she grabbed his hand to walk beside him on what would be one of the hardest days of his life, he fell right in sync.

The stench of staleness filled Monty's nostrils as soon as he stepped into the lobby of the control room. And although Cara tried to play it off as if it was nothing, he could tell that the smell bothered her too. After showing their IDs and filling out the visitor paperwork, a female officer had Cara follow her, while a male officer came for Monty. The search was a normal part of the procedure, so both of them had already expected it. Yet, it still made them uncomfortable. When it was over, they each walked out of the strip rooms and breathed a sigh of relief.

Once escorted inside the visitation room, Monty became even more nervous. Cara noticed and squeezed his hand, just to give him a little reassurance, but deep down, she was nervous too, maybe even more so than him. The pat search, although uncomfortable, was actually the easy part. The hardest was yet to come.

As Monty and Cara stood hand in hand and waited for his father to come out, Monty looked around at all the other faces. The room seemed to be filled with love and laughter, and Monty couldn't help but wonder if he would feel the same thing once he saw his father after so many years. Thankfully, he wouldn't have to wait long to find out.

"Excuse me, sir, the inmate you are here to see is at the assigned table waiting for you. I'll show you the way."

The guard's voice had pulled Monty from his thoughts and brought him back to reality. He then escorted Monty and Cara to the table they would use for the visit. To say that Monty's chest felt like it would explode was an understatement. He couldn't remember the last time his heart had beaten so hard and so fast. The thought alone made him sick to his stomach, but once again, Cara stepped in and made it all better.

"It's okay, baby. You got this, and I got you. Everything is going to be alright."

He glanced at her and smiled. When he looked forward again, his eyes landed on something familiar. Monty may have been very young when his father was taken away, but he could never forget the last time he laid eyes on him or the last words his father had spoken.

"Montana, I need you to understand that I'm going away for a very long time, but I need you to always remember that no matter what, I love you and will carry you in my heart. Maybe one day when you're older, this will all make sense, and I'll see you again. Please, don't ever forget me."

Monty had replayed those words over and over in his mind through the years, and it was only because of his mother that he didn't believe them. But he finally had the opportunity to find out if they were true. Monty nodded at his father and then pulled a chair out for Cara to sit in, then sat down himself. The situation was a little uncomfortable, and it seemed as if no one wanted to be the first to speak. Surprisingly, Monty broke the silence.

"Sup, pops? Bet you never thought you'd see me here sitting across from you."

Montel smiled and nodded at his son's words and responded.

"Actually, son, I thought the opposite. I knew in my heart that one day we would be reunited, and that day is finally here. I knew you'd probably have a lot of questions, and I'm ready to answer every one of them. You may not like some of the answers, but at least they will be the truth."

"It's really all good. I mean, between Uncle Taboo and Chance, I pretty much know all the important parts. I kinda just want to forget about the past and focus on what's ahead.

However, I wish someone would have told me I had a brother sooner. That's the only thing that bothers me."

"Ah, yeah. I always thought that you should know, but your momma refused to let Chance or anyone associated with him be in your life. If it wasn't for your uncle and help from acquaintances, I don't know what type of life your brother would've had. Even though it was before I met her, she was a jealous woman. I never messed around on her. How could I? She was the whole entire package, and I wish that she was still around to tell her. Anyway, enough about that for now. Who is this beautiful young lady you have with you? It seems as if I know her."

Monty scrunched his eyebrows and turned to look at Cara. It seemed so crazy to him that Chance and now his father claimed to know her from somewhere. Shit just seemed strange, but once again, Monty pushed it to the side.

"This here is my future wifey, Cara, and I seriously doubt you know her from anywhere. Just like me, you've been in here most of her life."

"I swear, I've seen those eyes before, but maybe I am just tripping. It sure is nice to meet you, though. However, if I'm not being too rude, I'd really like a few minutes alone with my son."

Monty couldn't believe that his father had the nerve to ask Cara to let them be alone, and he let him know it.

"The fuck you mean? She ain't got to go nowhere. We came here together, so anything you have to say to me, you can say in front of her. That's how we do."

Monty felt like his father had no say-so when it came to him or his girl, but Cara just wanted them to have peace with each other, so she pushed her chair out and stood.

"No, Monty, it's okay. I have to go to the ladies' room anyway, and besides, you two really need this time together."

Cara bent down and kissed Monty on the forehead, then nodded at his father before she walked off. However, no matter how okay it was with Cara, Monty was pissed about it, and he let his father know it.

"Look, you ain't even been back in my life for an hour yet, so don't try and dictate a damn thing when it comes to me or her. She's a part of me, and I don't hide shit from her."

Montel looked Monty in the eyes and nodded. He completely understood where his son was coming from, but he needed Monty to also understand him.

"Look, son, let me school you on something. No matter how we feel or how much we trust the women in our lives, they shouldn't be a part of what we got going on in the streets. Knowing too much could be used against them, and I'm not just talking by the crackers. I'm talking about the opps, and sometimes, even by our own people knowing things could be costly to them and to us. And from the look in your eyes when you look at that pretty little lady, you don't want anything to happen to her. So please, just go with me on this and keep her out of your business, and especially out of mine. You understand?"

"Yeah, I hear what you saying and all, but Cara is different. She's down for the cause, and ain't nobody dumb enough to fuck with her anyway."

"Really? Oh, 'cause you a gangsta now and people fear you? You saying that jack move that was pulled on her was just for show?"

"How the hell you know about that?"

"Oh, I see, you think, because I'm locked behind these gates, that I don't know and hear shit? Well, son, you're wrong. I'm not even tripping about that, though, because I know you're ignorant to who I was out there and who I still am in here. You can't even begin to imagine the reach of my power. It's okay, though. I respect your momma completely for doing what she could to shield you from my life, but there were certain things that you should've known to help you thrive out there in them streets."

"Oh, you talking about the same streets your brother pushed me out in? Fuck you. My momma did just fine by me, and you need to remember that when you talk about her."

"Montana, your momma was everything to me. From the first day I met her to the day I had to leave her, and I never put her in the middle of what I had going on out there. You know, she actually thought I was out there entertaining other women, and although she was enough for me, I let her believe that. I would rather she think that than jeopardize her. There was no way I could've lived with myself if she ended up in the same position I'm in now. As a man, that should be something you can understand and respect."

"Yeah, whatever. Why don't you just go ahead and tell me why I'm here so I can go? I got more important shit that I could be doing."

The words were a blow to Montel's heart, but he understood why Monty felt the way he did. He wasn't about to push him, though.

"Alright, I'll tell you why I asked you to come. Chance told me what happened between the two of you, and unfortunately, he had to end your relationship with his connect. I understand why he did it, because I would've done the same. Since that happened, I know that you have no way to pick yourself back up, and soon, you're gonna get desperate. Am I correct?"

"Somewhat, but I'm not that bad off. And anyway, I went and talked to Chance, and me and him done moved past all that. I'm sure that he will re-establish things on my behalf."

"That's what you think? Because that's not what's gonna happen, son. Shit just don't work like that in the game. Besides, just like Chance, you're my seed, and both of you should carry greatness. You are supposed to have your own thing going. Not something that someone else has the power to take from you. Chance is your brother, true enough, but he is also a businessman, and oftentimes, those two things don't mesh well together."

"So what is it that you want from me? You want me to beg you to call him so he'll put me back on? Well, you can kiss my ass on that one, because I ain't asking you for shit. I done my whole life without your guidance, so I'm sure I can cross the street now without you holding my hand."

Monty knew the words he spoke hurt, but it was what he felt at that moment. However, the truth was, he needed a new source or a lot of things would change in his life. He played hard because he didn't want his father to feel like he needed him, although he had no other options.

"You can be angry with me all you want, but the key to the streets is yours, and you will never have to beg me or anyone else for it. Now, when you get back to your car, call the number I had programmed into your phone. After that, everything else will fall into place."

"And what if I don't call it? Then what?"

"Then nothing. Continue to live your life as is, but know that the number will always be available. If you do call, keep that young lady out of it. I know those eyes from somewhere, and if my gut feeling is right, she's not who you think she is."

With that said, Montel walked away with the guard to go back to his cell, leaving Monty with a lot to think about. He was pretty sure that Monty would make the right choice, because after all, he was born a gangsta.

Chapter 10

Monty leaned his head back on the headboard and stared at the number that had somehow been programmed into his phone while Cara tried to work on his semi-hard manhood. He wasn't in the mood, though, so her effort was all for nothing. Monty was too focused on deciding if he was going to call the number or not, but he knew he had to make a decision, especially since Chance really wasn't going to re-establish his ties to the connect.

"Come on, Monty, stop being so selfish with the dick. That thing with your dad was nothing, so stop letting it bother you."

"See, that's where you're wrong, because what's bothering me is why you so damn familiar to mufuckas affiliated with me. I mean, that shit ain't just a coincidence. Is there something about you that I need to know?"

"I don't know. Maybe when they look at me, I remind them of someone else. Could you just stop trying to figure shit out and fuck me like I asked you to? A bitch needs to cum right now. And why you keep staring at that damn phone? You trying to sneak and text another bitch or something? If so, you need to let me know."

Monty took his eyes off the phone and looked at Cara. He had never seen that ghetto side of her, but it turned him completely off. Monty quickly pushed her away from him and sat up. He had dealt with enough bitches like that and wasn't about to be bothered with another one.

"I got some shit I need to tend to, and I'ma need some private time with it. I'll be back."

Monty stood from the bed and pulled up his Rocawear jeans while Cara smacked her lips behind him. If she had been any other bitch, he would've thrown her out, but because he had love for her, he let it slide, at least for the time being.

Once Monty was where he knew Cara couldn't hear him, he pushed dial on his phone, and although he didn't know what to expect from the other end, he knew he had to take that chance. He figured that shit in his life couldn't get any worse. After the phone rang several times, Monty decided to hang up, but before he pushed end, he heard a voice.

"Sup, Montana. This is Peanut. I been waiting for your call."

"Yeah? Well, I wonder why that is, since I literally just obtained your number, so you couldn't have possibly been waiting that long."

"Actually, I've been waiting years for your call. You just didn't know it until now. Why don't you take some time and see me so I can tell you what your father couldn't? Oh, make sure you come alone. I'll text you the directions."

The called party hung up and left Monty with a dial tone. Not even two minutes later, a text came through with directions. After Monty read the information, he made sure to delete it. He didn't need Cara to stumble upon it and question him, or anyone else for that matter.

"You coming back to bed or what? Unless of course you got to run to the bitch you just got a text from."

Monty heard Cara's voice from behind him and wondered just how long she had been there. He may never know, but one thing was for sure, she was getting on his last nerve, and it pissed him off.

"Yo, where in the fuck is all this ghetto-ass shit coming from? And don't tell me it's who you really are, because if it is, you gone find yourself right where Bella is. Gone."

"Oh, you think I'm acting different? Well, I could say the same thing about you, because ever since we got back from visiting your damn father, you been acting shady. You must have let him put something in your head that shouldn't be there."

"My father ain't got a damn thing to do with how I'm feeling, but it seems that he got you all riled up. What's up with that?"

"What's up is the way he dismissed me. I know I acted like it didn't bother me, but it did. Especially since I ain't never did anything to him."

When Cara put it like that, it made Monty feel guilty about continuing the visit after his father asked her to leave. Monty and Cara went there as a couple and they should've remained there as one.

"Come on, Cara. He just wanted some time with me, that's all. You made the choice to go out and wait in the car."

"Well, what else was I supposed to do? Stand by the vending machines and watch you from afar? Besides, if the shoe would've been on the other foot, you would've done the same thing."

"Well, since you think you know me that good, you know ain't a woman alive that could take your place. You in here doing all that tripping for nothing."

Monty pulled Cara into his arms and looked down into her eyes. He didn't give a damn about what anyone said about her. She was his queen, and only she could hold his attention so hard.

"I know, Monty, and I don't know what came over me. I usually don't get jealous because I know where we stand with each other. It's just that I'm so afraid someone will change your mind about me."

"Baby, you and I stand strong together and can't nobody change that, but right now, a nigga wants to lay down with your pretty ass. You cool with that?"

"Am I? Now you know I been trying to get the dick all night. It's you that's been stopping the flow."

Monty smiled and picked Cara up. He held onto her tightly as she wrapped her legs around his waist while he carried her back to bed. Once there, he laid her down and spread her legs so he could bury his face between them. He hadn't always been so quick to eat pussy, but with her, he just couldn't help himself. Cara was the sweetest thing he had ever tasted, and as he sucked on her swollen bud, he could hear her soft moans fill the room. Nothing made Monty more complete than giving her pleasure. Cara was the reason he woke up every day and why he came home at night. He would be damned if he allowed another mufucka to take that from him.

When Monty felt Cara tremble, he knew that she had reached her peak, but he wasn't letting up until every drop of her sweetness was on his tongue. When he finally came up for air, Cara pulled him down on the bed and wasted no time putting him inside of her.

"Damn, baby, you know you ain't got to rush it like that. This dick belongs to you and it ain't going nowhere."

"Oh, Monty, just shut up and let me fuck you."

Monty smiled and obliged, but as soon as he erupted inside of her, his cell phone buzzed and broke the mood. As bad as he wanted to ignore it, he just couldn't, but when he answered, he didn't like what he'd heard. Monty didn't even respond to the person on the other end, but instead, pushed Cara off of him and sat up.

"I got to go handle something. Stay here. I'll be back as soon as I can."

"What's so important that you have to rush out like that?"

Monty turned and looked at Cara with watery eyes. He found it hard to repeat what he had been told because it would make it even more real, but he knew that Cara was concerned.

"My brother's place just got hit, and they saying he ain't make it out. My people got a hold of one of the shooters, so I'm about to go make that mufucka talk."

"No, Monty, why can't you just let your crew handle it? What if something happens to you? You know Chance wouldn't want that."

"You wrong. It's what Chance would've expected me to do, because if it was me, he would reach out and do the same. That's my real fam, and to lose my life avenging his would be an honor."

Monty threw on his black Timbs along with his black Gucci jeans and hoodie. He then went in his closet and pulled out the same .45 Chance had given him years before. On his way out the door, he stopped and grabbed a bottle of Champagne. For some reason, it made it easier for him to take a life. Chance would always tease him about it and even dubbed him "The Champagne Killer," and although Monty's heart was split in two, he chuckled to himself when he thought about it.

Monty put the Champagne and his burner in a small duffle bag and jumped in his ride. He looked up and saw Cara as she stood in their bedroom window and watched him. He hoped that he would make it back home to her, but he also knew that once you go gangsta, life from day to day was no longer promised. Whatever happened would be what it was, and Monty was ready.

Monty pulled to the lakefront cabin his boy ReLay told him he would be at. When Monty got out, he was hesitant because ReLay's bitch stood on the front porch blowing bubbles with her gum like a bitch wasn't about to lose their life. She was a thick-ass redbone with a fucked-up attitude, and Monty couldn't stand her. He wondered why she was even there, because it made her a witness, and even ReLay knew what happened to those.

"He's in the back room waiting on you. All I ask is you hurry up and do what you need to do. I need my beauty sleep, and you holding me up. Oh yeah, and make sure you clean up after yourself, because I ain't your maid."

Monty gave her a strange look and wondered just how much ReLay had told her. Monty didn't want her up in his business and he planned to make sure ReLay knew it.

Monty walked to the back room of the house with a purpose. When he walked in, he saw a bright-skinned man tied to a chair in the middle of the floor. Monty could tell by his swollen lips and bloodied nose that ReLay had already roughed him up. He then noticed ReLay as he sat off in a dim corner in a leather recliner, with a nine-millimeter on his lap.

ReLay had been a young nigga fresh out of high school when Monty met him on the block one night. ReLay wanted to be a part of something major, but instead of choosing college, he chose the streets. Against Monty's better judgment, he gave him a spot on his team. Monty had never had an issue when it came to him, but bringing his bitch along on a job was about to change all that.

"While you sitting off in a corner chilling, all laid back and shit, you want to explain to me why your bitch is out there standing on the front porch? If I remember correctly, I told you how I feel about witnesses."

ReLay stood up out of respect for his mentor before he answered.

"My bad, Monty, but this her shit we up in. It was the only place I could think of to bring this mufucka to. Don't worry about her though. She cool and she ain't gone say nothing to nobody. I give you my word on that."

"Well, your word don't mean shit when you go against what I told you. Besides, you know I can't stand her ass."

"Well, if it will make you feel any better, I'll pull the trigger."

"Let's find out if one needs to be pulled first, and then we'll go from there."

ReLay had always tried to abide by what Monty spoke, but that one time, he had slipped up. He just wanted to step up and make Monty proud. Hopefully, in the end, it wouldn't cost him.

Monty reached into the duffle bag he had carried and pulled out the Champagne first. He had forgotten to bring a glass, so instead, he popped off the cork and downed it straight from the bottle. When he was done, he set the half-empty bottle on the floor and then pulled out the .45. It was already loaded with hollow rounds, his favorite ammo, but Monty made sure to push one in the chamber.

He turned and looked at dude to see his reaction, but there was none, and it pissed Monty off even more.

Monty pulled a chair up and sat in front of the man while his gun remained tightly in his grasp. He reached down and picked the Champagne back up and guzzled a little more. The sparkling brew seemed to clear his mind of everything besides what was in front of him. He always said he couldn't do a signature kill without his signature drink. The two of them just seemed to go together, and he dared anyone to challenge that.

"So, ReLay, you want to tell me who this mufucka is?"

"They call him Rocky 'cause his ass be over at the gym boxing and shit. I can't tell you when he became a hitman, though."

Monty nodded and looked Rocky right in the eyes before he spoke.

"So, Rocky, you felt like it was okay to knock down what my brother worked so hard to build? Then, you actually thought you was just gone walk away like shit smelled good, and you wasn't gone have to answer for it?"

Rocky stared at Monty but remained silent. Finally, ReLay walked over and handed Monty a picture along with a small piece of paper that an address had been written on.

"This a picture of his bitch and his ole' girl, along with the address of where they at. They home as we speak. All you got to do is give me the word, and Smash will take care of them. He's parked right outside their door right now."

Smash was ReLay's partner. They had been friends since the sandbox days, and when Monty pulled ReLay in, he let him bring Smash along. Together, the two of them were mufuckas, and they were also the most loyal of Monty's set.

Monty reached out and grabbed the photo and the piece of paper out of ReLay's grasp. He read the address out loud just so Rocky could hear just how real shit was, but when Monty looked at him, he remained expressionless. Monty decided to try another tactic.

"Shit. This bitch is fine. How long you all been together? 'Cause she don't look happy. I might need to tell Smash to hold off so I can go over there and put a real smile on her face. She look just like the type of bitch I like to run up in. Dick getting hard just thinking about it."

"Nigga, fuck you. My bitch would never lay down and give you the pussy."

"She don't have to, 'cause a nigga like me don't mind taking it. Turns me on more when they resist. Actually, momma's ass can get it too."

"Aye, I love my girl and all, but she can be replaced. My momma, though, she don't deserve that shit you talking. She ain't never did nothing to nobody."

"My brother Chance, he ain't deserve what he got either, and yet, he got it anyway. Ya girl, ain't no doubt about it, I'm fucking that bitch, but we may be able to come to some kind of compromise about ya momma. Depends on just how much you tell me."

"Look, I don't got much to tell you, but if you spare her, I'll give you what I can."

Monty stood up and walked closer to Rocky, and as he spoke, he walked in circles around him.

"I need to know if you running in on my brother was your idea or if someone else put you up to it, and when you answer, you better give me more than what you can, and you better feed me the truth."

"It wasn't my idea. I got the order from my boss, me and Crypto, but don't ask me who she is, 'cause I've never met her. That's the truth."

Monty stopped in his tracks and thought about what Rocky said. Unless his ears were playing tricks on him, he could've sworn that Rocky said "she," but he could've been mistaken. Monty needed to know.

"Did you just say 'she'? You got the order from a woman?"

"Yeah, that's what I said. I work for a female. What's the matter? You don't think women are capable of running shit and ordering kills?"

"Look, mufucka. I'm well aware of what women can do, so don't get cute, 'cause that will only piss me off even more, and right now, that ain't what you want, especially with dear old momma's life in my hands. Now, I need you to tell me who the hell you work for and who is Crypto?"

"Crypto is my partner. Well, he was, but he didn't make it out. That mufucka killed him right when he was taking his last breath, and I already told you that I've never met my boss, I've only ever spoken with her over the phone. I don't know what else you want me to say, 'cause I've told you the truth."

Monty balled up his fist and punched Rocky in the nose. He hit him so hard that the chair came up off of its front legs, but didn't topple over. Then Monty hit him again. Finally, the chair went down. Monty stood over Rocky and looked down at him. He found it hard to believe that a female put the hit out on Chance, but he had no choice but to go with what he was told.

Monty looked over at ReLay, who stood close by and waited for his orders. ReLay was a good, dependable soldier, and Monty truly liked the way he put in work. He was also grateful for how quickly ReLay responded and was on top of things to avenge Chance. Monty could do nothing but respect him for that.

"Yo, Lay, go head and put in that call to Smash. Tell him to go inside and get the mother. He can leave the bitch behind."

"A'ight, Bossman, I'ma do that right now."

When Rocky heard what Monty said, he panicked even more. He knew that he wouldn't be able to live with himself if something happened to his mother because of his own stupidity. Rocky had chosen to live the life he led, and he wasn't about to let her suffer for it.

"Wait, please. I gave you what you asked for. You can take my girl, but please, let my momma be."

Monty kneeled down so Rocky could hear him loud and clear because he didn't want to be misunderstood.

Rocky didn't know it, but Monty wasn't going to let anything happen to his mother. He only wanted information. Monty thought about his own mother and how he would feel if he was in the same position. He knew that he would plead for her too. Even lay down his own life to save hers, so the order Monty gave ReLay to make the call was only a bluff.

"Don't worry, I'm not going to let anyone hurt her, but I need you to understand that was my brother's life you took. If you two wouldn't have ran in on him, your partner would still be alive, so you can count your losses as even. Yo' momma, she ain't coming back until you give me a name or something else to identify who this so-called woman is."

"Fuck that, I told you all I knew. Just let her go."

"Like I already said, you tell me who it is you work for and I'll make sure she is returned, safe and sound. You, on the other hand, I can't promise."

"Come on, man, I don't know who she is."

"Well then, maybe I will have to hurt your mother. I'll give you a couple of days to think about it. I'm sure that's plenty of time."

Monty stood back up and slowly gathered his things, just to give Rocky enough time to think about the options. After he zipped up the duffle, he turned and looked at Rocky one last time, but just as Monty was about to walk out, Rocky had a change of heart.

Chapter 11

Monty followed the directions he had been given, although he wasn't sure what he'd stumble upon once he got there. He just hoped that whatever his father had set up for him would be worth the drive.

Monty had purposely scheduled his trip for that day so he would have a reason not to show up for the homegoing service that had been set up for Chance. Monty felt that as long as he didn't see Chance laid out in a casket, he could pretend he was still there and live his life as usual. He had already called and apologized to his uncle Taboo for his absence and let him know that Cara would show up on his behalf. Even though she knew Chance had never cared for her, she didn't argue and took Monty's place, respectfully.

When Monty pulled into the driveway of the house his GPS had led him to, he was a little taken aback. It was a small wooden house that looked like it would only take a strong gust of wind to knock it over. The paint that chipped from the wood panels made Monty sick to his stomach and threw him completely off. He looked at the number on the house and then at the address again. Sure enough, he was at the right place, so he parked his ride and got out.

When Monty walked up the steps that led to the front door, he hoped the concrete didn't crumble under his feet. Thankfully, he made it to the door safely, and once there, Monty breathed a sigh of relief and knocked. When the door opened, he was greeted by a cute white girl with a lot of attitude. With her hands on her hips, she gave Monty his answer before he could even ask the question.

"Peanut is over in the kitchen waiting on you, and just so you know, you're late."

The white girl walked off without another word and left Monty to fend for himself. Without directions, Monty shrugged and stepped inside. Usually, going to a strange place made Monty uncomfortable, and he would take his burner, but for some reason, he felt no fear and went unarmed. Once he found the kitchen, he was greeted by a nigga with dreads and a bottom grill.

"Sup, Montana? They call me Peanut, and I am so glad to finally meet you. I been waiting years for this meeting, and I know you have no clue why you're here, so I won't even beat around the bush. Come on and have a seat so I can fill you in."

Monty sat down at the table across from Peanut. He wasn't sure why, but he felt at ease in Peanut's presence. So at ease, he decided to ask him about the rundown shack they were in.

"It would be nice to know why Pops got me way the fuck out here with no kind of explanation, but first, can I ask why we in a dump like this? I mean, you look like you doing pretty damn good for yourself. You rocking name brands, sporting a gold grill, and I'm sure that diamond-encrusted Jesus piece you got around your neck cost you a nice grip, but yet, you in here crashing like a jugg."

Although Monty was serious, Peanut couldn't help but laugh. Had it been anyone else, Peanut might have felt disrespected, but he knew Monty meant no harm.

"I got to give you credit, you bold as a mufucka to question me about some shit like that, but this ain't where I lay my head. This place is actually yours. I've been using it as a deterrent for business purposes only. Perhaps one day, I can show you where I call home. Maybe we could meet up and have some drinks or something."

"That sounds straight, and look, I was just a little thrown off. I ain't mean no disrespect."

"Don't worry about it. I didn't feel offended. I know you meant well. Anything else you want to know before we get started?"

"Actually, what's up with the white girl that answered the door for me? She always have an attitude like that?"

"Oh, that's my baby, Kayla, and yeah, I guess you could say she a little ratchet, and she don't play about ya boy. I love that bitch, and once you get to know her, you'll understand why."

"Well, at least it's good to know that there's another side to her."

The two of them shared a laugh like two old friends, and then Peanut told Monty what he had been waiting to hear.

"You probably don't know this, but my pops and your pops were best friends and even business partners. Did almost everything together. They were a tight team, and it was hard for a mufucka to infiltrate them. That night everything went down, my father was killed. Luckily, yours is still breathing, maybe not free air, but at least his heart still pumps. I'd give anything to visit my father in a prison, rather than a grave, but I'm not that fortunate."

"Damn, bruh, I'm sorry for your loss, but my father might as well have died too because he wasn't around when I needed him to be. It's hard for a boy to grow up without his father around, and now, he thinks shit is sweet between us. You wanna tell me how I'm supposed to push on with that?"

"Look, I know it sounds crazy to say that the shit that happened wasn't his fault, but that raid put him in a bad position. They took out his best friend and wasn't no way he could let that slide."

"I know I done heard bits and pieces about that so-called jacked-up raid, but I don't know the whole story. Maybe you could break it down. Make me understand it a little better, maybe even explain to me why my pops ain't tell me himself. We were face to face, and it gave him every opportunity, and yet he ain't tell me shit."

"He couldn't tell you much of anything on that visit because the table you sat at was bugged. As hard as they tried to get him to give up his stash, he wouldn't do it. They even tried to make him a deal, but Montel stood strong. That raid was a fake, and somehow, your pops knew it was coming."

"So you saying, they didn't catch him with anything?"

"Nah, they ain't catch him and my pops with shit, and it made that crooked-ass FBI agent even angrier. That's how my pops lost his life. Wasn't the first botched raid he'd done either, it just ended up being the wrong one. Ran right in on our fathers while they were in the warehouse, the empty warehouse. Yours made it out, mine didn't. Your father didn't rest though, until he caught up with that fuck-ass agent, and once Montel found him, he shot him point-blank range between the eyes. Did it right in front of that bastard's four-year-old daughter. The agent also had an infant son lying asleep in his crib in the other room, but nothing was going to stop Montel from avenging my pops' murder."

"So what about the mother of the two kids? Where was she when everything went down?"

"The mother had died shortly after giving birth to the boy. She was fine one minute, and then the next she was convulsing. Died of cardiac arrest. Rumor has it, that one of the niggas her husband ran in on got some payback. It's never been proven, though."

"Damn, that's some real foul shit."

"Yeah, it was, and you would have thought it would stop his crooked-ass from that bullshit, but instead, they became more common. To him, every nigga in the hood was suspect. That was, until he ran up on the wrong ones that night."

"Hmmm. To think that my momma painted an entirely different picture almost pisses me off. Why in the hell wouldn't she just tell me the truth?"

"I don't know, but I'm thinking it was because she was trying to protect you. Maybe she wanted to make sure you went down a different road than your father did, but since you're sitting in front of me, that means her intentions didn't work."

"You right, I am here, and yet, I still don't know why."

"You're here to get the future that your father left for you. That's the only reason this house is still standing."

"Look, bruh, I appreciate you giving me a history lesson and all, but it's time to stop bullshitting, so I need you to go ahead and make this long-ass story short."

About that time, Kayla walked into the kitchen and gave Monty a sideways look. She didn't appreciate the way he was talking to her man, and she let him know it.

"Who in the hell do you think you're talking to like that? You better show some damn respect. Peanut is trying to help you, and here you go acting like an ass. Remember, he ain't got to do shit for you, so tighten up or leave and forget about it."

Monty was stunned by Kayla's boldness, but he liked the fact that she didn't mind standing up for her man. At first, when she had answered the door for him, he didn't like her fucked-up attitude, but after that outburst, he could only respect it.

"A'ight, shawty. I ain't mean to sound so harsh, but I got a lot of shit going on in my life right now, and I need to get back home and tend to it. So don't take shit so personal."

Peanut decided to speak up before Kayla had a chance to respond. He had grown used to her sticking up for him even though he could handle his own. Protecting him was something Kayla couldn't help, but sometimes it was uncalled for.

"Look, Montana, don't mind her. She just looking out for a nigga, that's all." Peanut then turned to Kayla and said, "Chill out, baby. My work is almost done. Besides, he didn't mean any harm. Now go ahead and get our things together so we can get up out of here."

Kayla smacked her lips and rolled her eyes but did exactly what Peanut said. As soon as she left the kitchen, Peanut stood and pulled a set of keys out of his pocket. He held them up and then handed them over to Monty.

"What am I supposed to do with these? You losing me right now."

"That is the key to this house. It belongs to you now. Years ago, I had one just like it a block over, and when I emptied it out, I had it demolished. I suggest you do the same."

"What? Come on now. I ain't catching what you saying. You gone have to break it down for me just a little bit better."

Peanut sat back down and explained.

"In the back room, there is a small closet. At the end of the clothes rack, there are three small screws holding it up. The screw on top is a fake. Push it and the floor will lower to an underground warehouse. Everything in there is yours and should have you set for the rest of your life. How you handle it and how you move it is up to you. I've kept it safe for you long enough, but if you happen to need me, you have my number."

With that said, Peanut stood and walked out. A few minutes later, Monty heard a car pull off. He couldn't believe that the nigga just up and left him on his own. Monty wasn't going to chase Peanut down, though. Instead, he decided to find that closet and see what all the fuss had been about.

Monty left the kitchen and located the back room. He was a little leery when he walked inside, but he didn't take Peanut for a snake, so he walked right over to the closet and opened the door.

The inside of the closet looked as normal as any other, with clothes hanging off of metal hangers and shoes that lined a shoe rack attached to the door. He knew that all of it had to have been staged and nodded his head at the smart move.

Monty stepped in the closet and pushed the clothes over to one side so he could see the end of the rack that held them. He pushed the top screw like he was told, but nothing happened, so he tried the other two. Still, there was nothing. Monty then pushed the clothes to the opposite side and pushed the top screw on that end. Suddenly, he could feel the floor beneath him move, and even though Peanut told him it would happen, he was still startled.

Once the floor had let all the way down, Monty stepped off the platform, and when he did, it went back up. Peanut never told him how to bring it back down so he could get out, but he would worry about that later. Monty looked around and saw a door at the end of the wall and approached it. When he walked inside, it was not what he expected, but even more.

Kilo after kilo lined the racks on the walls all the way around the room. On a table in the middle of the room were stacks of hundred-dollar bills along with a bill counter and a set of triple-beam scales. Monty was in complete awe because he had never seen that much cocaine or money in his life. Monty didn't know if he should rejoice or run, and when his cell phone vibrated, it scared the hell out of him because he was in such a daze.

He pulled the cell phone out of his back pocket and saw that it was Cara and smiled. He wished that he would have brought her so they could fuck right there and celebrate their future. He had dreamed of giving her the world, and now, it was finally within his reach.

"Sup, my queen, you missing me or something?"

"Yes, baby, I am. When you coming home? I really need you here holding me right now. Baby, I know that Chance couldn't stand me, but seeing him lying there in that casket done something to me. It brought back memories of my father too, and now, I just don't want to be alone."

"I know. That's why I couldn't do it. Ain't no way I could have stood there and looked at my brother, all helpless and shot. I would have been fucked up for the rest of my life. I appreciate you standing there for me, and when I get home, I'm a wrap your pretty ass in my arms, and when I do, I'm never letting go."

"Is that a promise? Or you just saying that to make me feel better?"

"Nah, baby girl. I'm a man of my word. I'll see you soon."

Monty hung up and thought about how Cara felt. For her to go and stand in on his brother's funeral for him meant more than she would ever know. He knew it would affect her in some type of way because no matter how Chance felt, he was as real as they came, and one could only respect that.

After Monty put his phone back in his pocket, he had to try and figure out how to get back up from the small underground warehouse. That was the one thing Peanut failed to mention. Finally, he found a switch by the door and flipped it, and a few minutes later, the closet floor came down. When it did, he breathed a sigh of relief and hopped on.

Monty looked around the house a little but found nothing of importance, except for a deed with his name on it. He put it in his pocket and then locked the house back up. He already knew that he would have to go and see his father again because he had so many questions. He just hoped that he would answer them. He remembered what Peanut had said about the table being bugged, but Monty knew very well how to talk in code, and he was positive that his father would understand.

Monty decided that once he got home, he would make love to Cara and then tell her what had happened, although he had been warned not to. He couldn't understand what the big deal was because she had yet to do him dirty. She had turned out to be the most loyal woman he had ever met, and he couldn't wait to truly spoil her and give her all she deserved. He felt like since Chance was gone, Cara was all he had. She was also the level-headed one in their relationship and would know just how to handle their newfound wealth.

Monty wondered if Chance had known about the stash house and if so, why he never told him. He couldn't worry about that though, because Chance was no longer around to ask him. Hopefully, the stash would be Monty's greatest come-up, because honestly, he couldn't stand another loss.

Chapter 12

ReLay sat in the passenger's seat of the dark gray Navigator while he and Monty shared a blunt. It was ReLay's first time smoking weed, and it made him feel like he was floating somewhere in space. ReLay was in celebration mode because Monty had promoted him to Lieutenant. Monty felt that since Dreybo was no longer around, he had to find someone else to help him handle all the street business. Since ReLay had put in the work and proven himself, he took the spot with a smile on his face.

At first, Monty had seriously considered giving Cara the spot, but since she was already his right hand, he gave it to ReLay instead, and he was so glad that he did.

"Damn, bossman, you ain't tell me this shit was gone have me feeling like an astronaut."

"Now come on, ReLay, that shit ain't got you like that, you just tripping 'cause you a virgin on it."

"That may be true, but I'll let you know where I'm not a virgin at."

"Nah, I'm good and uninterested in your dick stories, so you can keep those to yourself."

The fiends had been out heavy that night, and the downpour of rain wasn't about to stop them from getting their high on. Monty nursed on the fat blunt and watched the fiends in action. He was always ready to take their money, even though he no longer needed it. With all that his father had bestowed upon him, he could afford to stay at home and fuck his bitch all day instead of being out on the block, but Monty loved being out there and he felt like his presence alone made a difference. True enough, he could let his runners go out and do all the work, but he'd rather get his own feet dirty.

Shit was going good in his life, and he hadn't even touched the stash yet. Soon though, he would have to put his hands in it, and when he did, mufuckas better beware. He had plans to take over the whole hood and didn't care whose toes he stepped on when he did. His number one mission though was to find the bitch that put the hit out on Chance.

"Yo, Monty, bruh, you know I'm still putting the word out, trying to find out who the bitch is that put the hit out on Chance. I ain't gone even rest 'til that ho six feet deep."

"Thanks, ReLay, that's why I put you beside me, because you always looking out, and you a real ass nigga, 'bout the realest I ever dealt with. Chance would be proud to know that you sitting in his seat."

"Thanks, Boss, 'cause a nigga sure is glad to serve beside you. Smash too. He just don't like to be on the scene as much as I do."

"He still puts in that work, though, so it's all good. I knew I made the right choice from the first day I pulled you two in."

"And we gone forever be grateful. You know what I been thinking about lately?"

"Well, if it has anything to do with your dick, I don't want to know."

ReLay laughed and threw his hands up.

"Nah, I figured I'd save that story for another time, but on the real, I been thinking a lot about that night you and Dreybo got hit at the club. I was just wondering if you heard anything about who did it, 'cause we need to serve that justice for ya boy."

"Now you know had it been a direct hit on us, I would've found that mufucka, but that night, I think we just happened to go to the wrong club."

"Well, if that's the case, how come only you and Dreybo got hit? Well, other than that dancer he had pulled. Now she was in the wrong place at the wrong time."

Monty looked as if ReLay had lost his mind because he could've sworn that Cara told him there were several others killed in the ambush.

"You sure about that? 'Cause I heard something totally different."

"Come on now, Monty, I ain't that damn high. I know what I know and honestly, as much as I hate to say this, I think you was supposed to die that night too. If it wasn't for your girl, you'd be right there beside Dreybo in the ground."

Monty thought about it for a minute and then wondered why Cara hadn't told him the truth. He would make sure to ask her about it when he got home.

"ReLay, why you bringing this up now, when that shit happened a while ago?"

"Because I think that incident and the hit on Chance came from the same place. My gut's telling me that whoever this woman is, she angry as a mufucka."

"Well, if that's true, we gone find her and show her just what *angry* is."

"Damn right we are, and I'm a leave that ho the same way I left Rocky, mufucking heartless."

From out of the darkness, Bella appeared and knocked on Monty's window. It startled him at first, but once he realized who it was, he chilled and lowered his window. Monty was shocked to see her because she had been ghost ever since he dissed her for Cara.

Bella stood there looking finer than a mufucka in a pair of Victoria's Secret sweatpants and t-shirt. As always, she didn't have a bra on and her nipples were harder than stones. Monty couldn't lie to himself, he loved the hell out of Cara, but he often missed his little sexcapades, especially the ones with Bella. There was just something about her Spanish pussy that made his dick want to put in overtime.

"Hola, Papi. I see your bitch let you out of her sight for a minute, and that's all the time Bella needs to give you what you miss."

Monty licked his lips and smiled at her. Bella's accent made him rock up instantly, and as much as he wanted to send her away, he couldn't.

"Damn, Bella, you looking good as a fat juicy T-bone right now. Where the hell you been at?"

"Bella stay wet and juicy, even after you made me leave. I been waiting for you to return because I know she no give you pussy good as me."

Monty was so engrossed in Bella's sex appeal that he forgot all about ReLay, who still sat in his passenger seat.

"Yo, Monty, I know you ain't gone fuck with Bella like that while ya girl sitting at home. If Cara finds out, she gone kick that ass."

Monty turned his head to look ReLay in the eyes. He knew that ReLay was just looking out for him, but that night he was going to have to look out for someone else.

"What's the matter, Lay? You getting jealous over there? 'Cause if so, I'm sure Bella wouldn't mind including you too."

"Well, now that you put it that way . . . What ya girl don't know won't hurt her. Right?"

"Now we talking, besides, the only people that are going to know is you, me, and Bella. Ain't that right, Bella?"

"Yes, Papi, and you know Bella no say nothing to nobody."

"Go on and hop in the back seat, and soon as you get in, take all that shit off."

Bella quickly got in before Monty changed his mind and stripped just like he told her to do. She decided that she didn't mind giving the pussy to ReLay too because she was willing to do anything to get back in Monty's good graces.

When ReLay looked in the back seat, Bella was naked and ready for whatever came her way, and when she noticed he was watching her, she spread her legs and put on a show. Although, Bella fucked all flavors, she preferred black men. She just felt like their dick game was more solid than others.

"What's the matter? You never see a bitch play with her own pussy?"

"Nah, not a bad bitch like you."

"Hmm, well if you see a bad bitch, fuck her."

ReLay raised his eyebrows and then looked at Monty. He knew that Monty said they could both have her, but out of respect, he still wanted to make sure.

"You good, Lay? Go on back there and give her what she asking for. Shit, a nigga ain't even mad. I'ma catch this flow while you handle your business."

"A'ight, Bossman. That's what's up?"

ReLay crawled into the back seat where Bella was at, and before he could get his jeans all the way to the floor, she had his dick in her mouth. He didn't even try to finish taking them off because Bella had him in a choke hold. ReLay's eyes rolled in the back of his head as Bella swallowed every inch of his manhood. It was the best head he ever had, but ReLay wanted the pussy, so he pushed her up off of him.

"What's wrong? You no like the way Bella give you head?"

"Shiiit, Bella, you sucking this dick better than I could have dreamed, but I'm ready for something else. Come on and boot that thang up so a nigga can get in it."

As soon as Bella got on all fours and put her ass up, ReLay went in and put in that work. Monty could only shake his head. He sat and listened to Bella moan while ReLay went deep and talked that shit to her. The two were so fixated on what they were doing, that they didn't even notice when Monty got out, and as soon as he did, a fiend approached him.

"Hey, Monty, you think you could let me hold a little something 'til payday next week?"

"Next week? What in the hell happened to this week?"

"I had to get me a few snacks and some more candles. Plus, I owed out the rest of it, but next week's check is clear and you can have it all if you do me a solid."

LaRia was one of the few crackheads that brought home a paycheck. She had somehow managed to hold down a job at Walmart for a little over a year, all while nursing her addiction. LaRia lived in a Section 8 apartment with no electricity, and the only reason she had running water to bathe her ass in was because she would give the water meter man head whenever he came around.

"You got you some electricity yet or you just gone keep using up them candles?"

"What I need electricity for? I see just fine with those candles and I don't mind taking cold showers either. That ain't for you to worry about, though."

"Yeah, you right but damn, don't you get tired of living like that?"

"Look, are you going to let me hold something or not, 'cause I need a hit right now and you keeping me from it."

"Yeah, I'ma let you hold something, but don't make me come looking for you about my bread. You know a gangsta trying to come up and shit and I need every penny I can get."

"Whatever, Monty, you know I'ma pay you, and stop acting like you ain't doing big things. You driving around here in a brand new Navigator with twenty-inch rims. Wearing that Diamond face Rolex and you worried about a few measly dollars. Don't let me find out you petty."

"Go 'head on with that shit, LaRia. I'ma need my money like I said. Everything else is irrelevant."

Monty reached in his pocket and pulled out a package that held fifteen medium-sized pieces of crack and handed it to her. He just wanted to get rid of her before she noticed that Bella and ReLay were in his back seat, but little did he know, she had already peeped it.

"I'ma pay you, Monty, but what you should be worried about is Bella in your back seat. I don't care if it's not you she's fucking. That bitch is grimy and I hope your girl beats her ass."

No sooner than LaRia said it, Cara pulled up in her silver BMW and parked in front of the Navigator. He looked at LaRia, who in turn, smiled and walked away. Monty knew there was no way he could get Bella out of his truck before Cara realized she was there.

Cara usually never showed up on the block while Monty was out hustling, so he was a little put off by her presence. He knew that he had to try and act as normal as he could, but Cara wasn't one to be easily fooled.

"Sup, baby? Why you out here like this? I told you I wouldn't be out long, why don't you go head back home and I'll see you there?"

Cara looked at him strangely because it felt like he was trying to get rid of her. However, it didn't take her long to figure out why. Cara heard Monty's door open and shut and looked towards his Navigator. When she looked back at Monty with an attitude, he knew shit was about to hit the fan.

"What in the hell is that bitch doing getting out of your back seat? Huh, motherfucker? Is that why you're trying to get rid of me?"

"Baby, please just chill. She ain't with me, she's with ReLay. That's why I was standing outside the truck when you pulled up. You got to believe me."

Cara looked at Monty again and then turned and rushed Bella. She hit Bella so hard, she could've sworn she broke a knuckle. ReLay jumped out of the Navigator at the same time Monty ran to Cara in hopes of stopping the ass whooping Cara was putting on Bella. They knew they had to gain control of it before the police showed up, but unfortunately, they didn't stop it in time, and as soon as the police pulled up, both Monty and ReLay threw their dope in the bushes. When they did, LaRia rushed over and grabbed their packages. Little did they know, she had seen Cara turn down that block and already knew what would happen, and when things turned out just as she had planned, she called the police. After she grabbed their packages, she secured them in her bra and went on her way.

The police had to mace Cara to get her off of Bella, and since it seemed as if Bella never hit back, Cara was the only one they arrested. Monty shook his head and promised her that he would be there to get her out as soon as they gave her a bond. She apologized to Monty for acting out and then got in the back seat of the police car. After the officer drove away with his woman, Monty turned to Bella and gave her a piece of his mind.

"You stupid bitch. What the hell was you thinking when you got out? Huh? I know you saw her out here. You ain't think she wasn't going to beat your ass?"

Through the pain that she felt all in her face and bloody lips, Bella smiled. She wasn't studying Monty's ass. She had gotten just what she wanted—some good dick and some payback.

"Fuck you, Monty, I don't care about how your bitch feels because she didn't care about how I felt when she pushed me out of your life. Both of you were wrong for that. You thought I had no feelings when I had plenty, but now, I owe you no respect. And as far as your dick game is concerned, your young friend here has you beat."

With that said, Bella looked over at ReLay and winked, then walked away, right back into the darkness she had come from. She hadn't been the least bit embarrassed by getting her ass beat because things turned out just as she had wanted them to.

When Bella was out of earshot, ReLay walked over to Monty and apologized.

"Aye, Bossman, that's my bad. I ain't even realize ya girl had pulled up."

"Yo, good, ReLay. Bella's ass knew exactly what she was doing. I'm a need you to push the Nav to my house, though, 'cause it looks like I'm a have to drive Cara's car home."

"Now, you know I got you, but first, I'm a go head and grab those packages from the bush. We can't leave those behind."

"Yeah, you go ahead and handle that while I grab my phone out of the truck."

ReLay walked over to the bush that they had thrown their packages in and looked around, but nothing was there. He knew it was the right bush because they used the same one every time. He scrunched his eyebrows together and checked it again. Still, nothing. Monty noticed that something was off because ReLay was taking too long. So he walked over to the bush to find out what was up.

"Aye, ReLay, what's taking yo' ass so long? We need to get the hell up out of here so I can go find out what's going on with Cara. What you doing?"

"Shit's gone, Monty. I've looked everywhere around this damn bush but can't find it."

"The fuck you mean it's gone? That's the bush we threw it in. It has to be there."

"Well, I'm telling you that it's not. If you don't believe me, you can check it for yourself."

Monty couldn't believe that someone had got them for their packages, but it was true, and he knew it could have been only one person.

Chapter 13

The product Monty had left over from when he worked for Chance had started to dwindle to practically nothing, so he had to make plans to take a trip back to the house his father had left him. He had waited as long as he could to touch it, but he needed both, the drugs and the money, as soon as possible. Monty had made plans to invest some of the money the way Chance had done and felt like it would be a way to honor his fallen brother.

Monty didn't want to take the long drive by himself, but he also didn't want to take Cara. Ever since that night she jumped on Bella and got booked, she had been salty toward him. Even held back on the pussy. It was cool though, because Monty planned to ask ReLay to take the ride with him instead. Of course, ReLay quickly agreed.

"Aye, bossman. Now I know I agreed to take this ride with you, but you ain't tell me that you was taking me through redneck country. You knew them white boys be tripping when they see a nigga on they turf. Shit, I don't know about you, but I ain't up for no attack."

"Come on now. You really think I would take you somewhere that would put you in harm's way? You tripping, because all of these fields and fancy farms out here belong to the black man, and once you see what I got going on, you'll be glad you came."

"What? You said all this belongs to our people? That's what I like to hear, because we damn sure deserve it, and since you put it like that, you can tell them white boys to kiss my ass."

"Nigga, you is crazy. That's why I like having you around. Now lean on back and take a nap or something while I drive. I'll wake you up when we get there."

"That sounds good, bruh, but let me warn you ahead of time, I do snore."

Monty just laughed at ReLay's comment and kept driving, and not even ten minutes later, ReLay's snores filled the inside of the Navigator. Not even the smooth sounds of Giveon could drown it out. Monty could deal with all types of noise, but snoring wasn't one of them, so he punched ReLay in the arm and woke him up.

"Damn, mufucka, you said you snored, but I ain't know you meant like that. Wake your ass up. We about to pull in anyway. Up in my shit sounding like a bear. Fuck is wrong with you?"

"I tried to warn your ass, but no, yo wanted me to take a nap like I'm a child or something, so that's on you."

"Well, I know next time. Matter of fact, how 'bout on the way back, you drive and I'll take a nap."

ReLay just shook his head and looked out the window. The trees that lined the street suddenly became thicker, and the paved road turned to dirt. A few minutes later, Monty pulled into the driveway of his newly inherited property. When ReLay saw it, he had the same reaction Monty had when he first went there.

"Yo, what the hell is this? You playing games with me, bruh, or you done got us lost?"

"No, nigga, we exactly where we supposed to be, so go 'head and get out and grab those duffle bags from the back while I open the door. Make sure you meet me inside. And Lay, don't take too long. I'm trying to get in and get out as quickly as possible."

"A'ight, damn, but I'm telling you, something don't feel right."

ReLay shrugged and got out. He pulled the six duffle bags Monty had brought out of the back of the Navigator.

With an uneasy feeling in his stomach, he walked to the front steps and stopped. ReLay didn't know why, but the place spooked the hell out of him. He hoped that whatever Monty had stashed there would all be taken that day, because he never wanted to step foot on that property again.

"ReLay. Nigga, why you just standing there like a zombie? Let's move. I ain't trying to be here all night."

The sound of Monty's voice startled him, and when he walked up the steps, he stumbled. ReLay felt a little embarrassed about the fall, but he picked himself up and pressed on anyway. Thankfully, no one else had seen it. ReLay walked inside but didn't see Monty, so he called out to him.

"Monty, this shit ain't funny. Where the hell you at?"

"In the back bedroom where you should be, mufucka."

ReLay followed Monty's voice until he found the back bedroom Monty was in. ReLay was just ready to get whatever over with so they could leave because with each second that passed, he was feeling more and more uneasy.

"I hope that whatever we came here for is worth all this damn trouble."

"Oh, I can assure you, it's worth more than that. Come on now and get in this closet with me."

"The closet? Hell no. Now that's where I'm drawing the mufucking line at. I know what happens in closets and it ain't pretty. You go ahead. I'm a be right here when you step back out."

"Come on, ReLay, your ass is tripping about nothing. This right here ain't no ordinary closet. Now bring your ass on so we can get what we came for. The sooner we get it, the sooner we will be gone."

As much as he was against it, ReLay went ahead and stepped into the closet along with Monty. A minute later, he felt the floor lower. Monty looked at him and smiled and then had to ask.

"How the hell you a damn killer, but your ass is afraid of a closet? What if you had to stake a mufucka out in one?"

"Well, I guess the nigga would still be breathing, and besides, this closet ain't got shit to do with my killing tactics. I done seen people get beat, starved, and even raped in one of the mufuckas, so I'm anti-closet and that's just the way it is."

"Ain't you got closets at your place?"

"Damn right, I do, but ain't none of them got a door. I ain't taking a chance at someone catching me off guard."

"Man, come on and get off of here."

About that time, the floor stopped, and Monty stepped off. ReLay was still hesitant, but he stepped off behind him. He made sure to stay as close to Monty as he could get. He hoped nothing happened to where he needed his gun because his hands were full. Hopefully, Monty was strapped too. At least that would bring him a little peace of mind.

ReLay followed Monty all the way to the door, and when Monty opened it and went inside, he walked in behind him, but when he looked around, he was confused at what he saw.

"Check me if I'm wrong, but this room looks empty to me. You sure you at the right place?"

Monty looked around and couldn't believe what his eyes told him. The small warehouse was completely empty. Not one brick of cocaine was left, nor one stack of money. Monty didn't understand what could have happened or who was behind it. Other than him and Cara, and ReLay who just found out, no one else knew about the stash house. No one except for Peanut and Kayla. Peanut didn't put Monty in the mind of someone who would pull a jack move like that, but then again, it could have all been a front. However, Monty couldn't think of anyone else to put it on.

"Nah, ReLay, you ain't wrong. Somebody done came in here and cleaned me out, and I think I know just who it was."

"Well, what we waiting on? Let's go put some holes in that mufucka and take that shit back."

"Uh uh. That's exactly what he's expecting me to do, and he's probably already set up and waiting for me to show. I'm a have to sit back and wait this shit out for a minute. My brother always told me not to move too fast because it could cost me more than money and drugs. I just hate that I waited so long to listen."

"So we done came all this way to pick up some shit that somebody else done beat us to and we ain't gone do nothing about it? That's some pussy ass shit right there, Monty."

"That's okay, it can be puss for now, because it's going to get gangsta later on. Now let's get out of here so I can try and plan our next move."

"A'ight, boss, but remember when you ready to make that move, me and Smash got your back."

Monty nodded and walked out of the room. ReLay threw his hands up and followed behind him. He hated to see his boss in such a funk, but he had a good reason to be.

Monty and ReLay left the house, and had a quiet drive home. ReLay tried to put in a Mike Smiff track, but Monty quickly shut him down. He needed a peace of mind so he could think straight. He needed to figure out how to play his next hand. A mufucka was going to have to answer for his shit, because that was a violation he refused to leave unpunished.

On the drive through the block to ReLay's house, Monty spotted LaRia and pulled over. At first, he was going to take what she stole as a loss, but Monty needed his shit and he was going to make that bitch pay. ReLay was confused as to what was going on, but Monty quickly informed him.

"That bitch is the one who stole our packages out of the bush. She thinks she got away with it, but I need my shit back."

"Now, how are we going to get that back? You know that bitch done smoked all of it up by now, talking about when she gets paid."

"Fuck that. I done lost enough. I'm tired of mufuckas thinking they can just take from me and it's all good. I'm gone have to make an example so that bitch is either gone give me my shit or she gone eat a hollow point for dinner. Her choice."

Monty jumped out of his ride and ran up on LaRia without her even knowing it. She didn't realize anyone was behind her until Monty grabbed a handful of her weave.

"Let me go, you motherfucker, or I'ma scream."

"Bitch, where the hell is my shit? And don't tell me you wasn't the one who took it 'cause I already know the truth."

When LaRia realized it was Monty who had a hold on her, she calmed down and her whole attitude changed. She figured that when it came to him, she could con her way out of anything and any other time, it might have worked, but that was definitely the wrong time.

"Oh my God, Monty. I ain't gonna lie. I saw you throw it in that bush, you and your friend, and I knew it was only because the police had showed up. I figured I'd help you out and pick it up, ya know, hold it until you came back around looking for it, but you didn't come back. Thought that maybe you wasn't worried about it, so I took care of it myself."

"That's a bad lie, LaRia, 'cause you knew you never had any intentions of giving my shit back. Now I'm a give you two minutes to give me my dope, or my money. Either one is fine by me, but you gone produce something, or we gone have a serious problem."

"Come on, Monty. Just give me 'til next week when I get paid again, and you can have my whole check."

"Hell no. You pulled that same game on me last week. I ain't falling for that shit again."

"But I had to pay my water bill with it. Old Jimmy don't work at the water company no more, so if I want to keep bathing my ass, I gotta pay the money. On the real, Monty, just give me 'til next week and I got you."

"Bitch, fuck you and next week. I'ma teach you about trying me like a soft ass nigga. You can keep next week's check, 'cause you gone need it to pay for your funeral. Handle that for me, Lay."

Monty went and got back in his ride while ReLay took care of LaRia. After ReLay got back in the Nav, he looked at Monty and nodded, and then they drove away, leaving LaRia with her head leaking.

After Monty dropped ReLay off at home, he drove the speed limit until he pulled up in his own driveway. When he walked in, Cara was sitting on the stairway waiting. It was as if she already knew he would need her. Everything she had been through for the last week was put aside just so she could be there for Monty. She was just real like that.

"Come on, baby. Come tell me all about it."

Monty smiled at her and grabbed her hand. Together, the two of them walked up the stairs and into their bedroom. Monty sat down on the bed while Cara went and ran a hot bath. He couldn't wait to submerge himself in the water with Cara sitting in front of him, and as soon as he heard the water cut off, he got undressed and met his woman in the bathroom.

Cara was already undressed, and when Monty walked in, he took a moment to admire her curves. He didn't know how he had got so lucky to have a woman like her. Damn what anyone else thought. Monty leaned down to kiss her while she stood on her tiptoes and met his lips, and then they got in the water. Monty held her close and told her about his day.

"That mufucka got me for everything. I know it was him, and he gone get his, mark my words."

"Monty, you can't just go around killing people because they wronged you. Sometimes, you just got to be the better man and walk away."

Monty looked at Cara as if she'd lost her mind, and who knows, maybe she had.

"Walk away? Hold up. What have you done with my woman, because you damn sure don't sound like her."

"I'm just saying, baby. Killing him is not going to get your product or money back, so what's the use?"

Monty knew that she was right, but he was a gangsta and there was no way he could let that shit go. He suddenly wished that Chance was there to guide him, but since he was gone, he could only think of one other person who would know what to do. As soon as Monty woke up the next day, he planned to go see them.

Chapter 14

The visitation room was just as crowded as it was the first time Monty went there, but at least, the pat search was as uncomfortable. It was actually almost as if, the guard didn't want to do it, but did it anyway for the cameras.

Monty had decided to go and see his father again before he made another move. He thought it would be best to check with him and find out the best course of action, and because of that, he went alone. He knew that if he had took Cara, his father would say nothing and he didn't want to take that chance.

Monty finally saw his father being escorted out of the inmate entrance by a different guard than the last time. Once the guard sat his father down at a corner table, he went and got Monty. The vibe seemed off though, and Monty hoped that was a good thing.

When Monty got to the table, he nodded and smiled at his father, then sat down. As soon as the guard walked away, Montel began.

"Don't worry, son. He works for me and he made sure that he assigned us a secure table so we could talk freely."

"I don't understand. You're already locked up, what more could they want from you?"

"My soul if they could get it, but it's too late because the devil already has it. Anyway, first things first. Did you empty out the house yet? If not, I want you to do so as soon as possible, and then, I want you to burn it down. Do you understand?"

"Yeah, I understand. The house is empty, but pops, it wasn't me who cleaned it out. Somebody else beat me to it."

"What the hell do you mean, somebody beat you to it? Nobody else should have known about it. Son, I worked years to build that for you and now you sit here and tell me that someone took it."

"Yeah, that's what I'm saying. I think it was that nigga Peanut and his bitch."

"No, I can tell you for sure that it wasn't him. He's had control of it for years. If he wanted it, he could have taken it, but yet, he watched over it until he could pass it to you."

"I don't know, pops. I don't know. Ain't nobody else I can think of, unless that mufucka told somebody. Shit, all I know is that it's gone and now I'm down to nothing. The fuck am I supposed to do?"

Montel leaned back and looked around the room. He had to think for a minute because things just wasn't adding up. He had worked hard for so long to be able to provide Monty with a future, and to think that someone had the nerve to take it from him had him pissed off. When Montel leaned forward again, he looked even more serious than the question he asked.

"Who did you tell about the house? And don't tell me that it was no one, because that stash has been under there for many years, but no one fucks with it until you know about it. You want to tell me how that is?"

"I didn't tell anybody, you told me not to, remember?"

Montel knew that Monty was lying because his right eyebrow twitched the same way his did when he lied. It was good to know that Monty at least inherited something from him. Montel only wished that it would have been something else.

"Ya know son, ya momma used to always know when I would come to her with a lie. I couldn't for the life of me figure out how she knew I was lying, until one day, she pointed it out."

"Oh yeah? Damn, that's fucked up, but how did she know?"

"Well, when I would lie to her, my right eyebrow would twitch, kinda like yours just did. So tell me the truth. Who did you tell about the house?"

"I told my girl. I just felt like she should know. I mean, she the one I'm gone spend my life with, and I didn't think that I should keep it from her."

Montel shook his head in disbelief. He was so disappointed in Monty that he had a good mind to get up and leave, but the only thing that kept him there was his word not to abandon Monty again.

"I thought I told you not to ever involve your woman in your business and yet, you go against what I say."

"I felt like she had a right to know, but I know she ain't had nothing to do with my shit being jacked. That shit has Peanut and his bitch written all over it. I'm telling you, pops, I feel it."

"And I'm telling you that your feelings are wrong. Damn it, son, when I tell you not to do something, don't go against it. I'll send a word out and get you a name, but it's gonna be up to you to get your shit back. From this day on, do not, under any circumstances, go against what I say. Do you understand me?"

Monty nodded. He wasn't happy about being scolded, but he deserved it. His father had warned him about talking too much to Cara, and even though he knew she had nothing to do with it, he still should have listened. He made a vow, from that day on, to keep things to himself.

"Yeah, pops, I do understand, and I can assure you. It won't happen again, but what do I do now? My shit is low. I need some type of re-up."

"I'll tell you what. When I go back to my cell, I'll put a call in to Peanut. He will contact you afterwards, so be ready. And son, keep it to yourself, because after this, my hands will be tied."

About that time, the guard walked up and ended their visit.

"Let's go, Hardy. Your time is up."

Montel stood and nodded at Monty, then walked away with the guard. He would make the call to Peanut as soon as he could get to a phone. He just hoped that he wasn't making a mistake by doing so.

Monty got in his ride and hoped that his father could get him back on, because if he didn't get something quick, he might have to make a jack move, and that was something Monty didn't want to do, especially since Dreybo was no longer around. He was certain that ReLay wouldn't mind stepping in, but he really didn't want it to come to that.

When Monty was about to pull into his driveway, his phone buzzed. The text only had an address, but Monty knew exactly who it was, so instead of pulling into his residence, he kept pushing the gas. He hoped Cara didn't notice because he didn't want to have to think of a lie to tell her.

Monty couldn't believe his eyes when he pulled into the driveway of the large brick home. The landscape was professionally done and should have won the yard of the week every week. The two-story home was charcoal gray in color and had bright white shutters on the windows. Monty got out and admired its beauty. True enough, he had his own mini mansion, but the one he looked at put his to shame. Peanut and Kayla's house should have been featured on *The Lifestyles of the Rich and Famous* because their shit was definitely on point.

Peanut walked out onto the closed-in porch and startled Monty, who still stood there in awe.

"Still think I live like a jugg?"

Monty heard Peanut's voice and looked up. He shook his head and laughed at the way Peanut used his words against him.

"Hell nah. If this is how a jugg lives, I'm about to change my profession. This place is nice."

"Thanks. Had it hand-built just the way I wanted it. Those charcoal gray bricks weren't easy to come across, but it worked out in my favor in the end. I mean, I did have to send Kayla in to do a little sweet talking, but it was damn sure worth it."

"Yeah, it was worth it. Hopefully, one day, I can upgrade my little space and do something big for me and Cara."

"You never know, but first, you gotta do things right. Can't spend everything you get. You gotta do some investing and then build from there. That's how you grow in this life."

"Damn, you sound like my brother. Makes me kinda feel like he's here still guiding me."

"Yeah, I'm sorry to hear about Chance. Do you know who did it yet?"

"Well, not exactly. I mean, dude that pulled the trigger already got his karma, but I'm still looking for the bitch that ordered the hit."

"Don't give up, Monty. Everybody gets theirs in the end. Now come on inside. Kayla done made some dinner that'll make you slap somebody."

Monty laughed and walked in the house behind Peanut. The view on the inside was even more grand than the outside. Monty took it all in so that when he got back on top, he could fix his shit up to match kingpin status. He felt like Cara was his queen and she should be living like one.

"A'ight, Peanut. Who's your decorator? I might need to hire them for my house."

"All this was Kayla's doing. She's got an eye for top quality, and she refused to let anyone else do it. I tried to hire a company to come in, but baby girl wasn't having it. Kinda glad now that I listened to her."

"Hey, ya thinkin' she would mind doing a little something with mine?"

Kayla walked up and answered before Peanut had a chance to. She didn't care much for Monty because although he professed to be gangsta, to her, he seemed weak, and she couldn't stand weak-ass men.

"Why your bitch can't decorate your house? Something wrong with her skills?"

Monty didn't like the way Kayla said it, so he spared her nothing.

"Hell nah, ain't a damn thing wrong with her skills, with your angry ass. Your parents ain't never taught you how to handle a compliment?"

"My parents taught me enough to know that I ain't doing the work another bitch should handle. She lay her ass there. Let her do it. Oh yeah, and dinner's ready."

Monty looked at Peanut to save him, who in turn, only threw his hands up and walked away. Monty shook his head and followed behind him to the dining room where a table full of food sat. Kayla looked from Peanut to Monty and pointed at their chairs. The two of them then sat down and enjoyed a plate of complete fulfillment.

Monty had to give Kayla her props, because the white girl could definitely cook the hell out of some soul food. He feasted on crispy fried chicken, homemade macaroni and cheese, collard greens, corn on the cob, and Jiffy cornbread. For dessert, Kayla served a mean pineapple upside-down cake. Monty hadn't had a meal like that since his momma died, and even though Cara could cook, Kayla had her beat, hands down.

When the meal was over, Monty swore he had *niggaritis*, because his ass was suddenly sleepy. He knew that happens after a good meal, but he also knew that he had gone there for business, and Peanut was ready.

"Come on, Monty, we gone go down to my man cave and talk about some things while my baby here does her womanly things."

Kayla rolled her eyes because she hated it when Peanut called cleaning up, "womanly things." Sometimes, she would guilt-trip him into doing the dishes and other household chores to show him it wasn't just for women. The only problem was, he did a half-ass job.

Peanut and Monty walked down the stairs to a man cave fit for a king. A one hundred-inch television hung on the wall at the front of the room with surround speakers in each corner. Monty could tell right away that Peanut was a Miami Dolphin fan because of all the Dolphin merchandise that filled the walls. Even the curtains had the Dolphins symbol on them. Monty himself had never cared for any of the Florida teams, but he wasn't about to knock Peanut for his taste.

As soon as the two of them sat down, Peanut got right to business.

"So your pops called and said you needed something to work with, but I gotta ask. What the hell happened to all the product and money I gave you the keys to? Ain't no way you done went through all that."

"Honestly, Peanut, I can't tell you what happened, because I don't know. I went back to take some out and the place was empty. I ain't gone lie either. I thought it was you who took it."

"Now that's funny, because I've had the keys to that place for a long time. Don't you think that if I needed that shit, it would have been gone?"

"That's what my pops said too, but I ain't know who else to blame. All of it, gone before I even had a chance to live my life off of it."

"Well, not trying to down you or anything, but from what I've been told, you jumped off the porch at fifteen, and all you got to show for it is a Navigator, a nice little place to call home, and a dime piece that drives a Benz. The hell did you do with all your shit? Ten years in the game and you really ain't got a damn thing to show for it. Now, I know Chance taught you better than that."

"He did teach me how to invest so that way, if something like this happened, I'd still have a future, but I ain't listen."

"And now look at you. I know it took a lot for you to go to your father and ask for help after things happened the way they did."

"Hmm . . . yeah, it did, but I didn't have anyone else I could go to."

"It's all good, because luckily for you, I have plenty, and I respect anything your pops ask me. It's because of him I live the way I live. My advice, though, is to take your money and put some away for the future. I understand that once you go gangsta, you wanna shine, but take my advice. That bright light will one day blow."

"I get what you saying and I respect that."

"Good, because it shouldn't be any other way."

Peanut stood and left the room. A few minutes later, he returned with three duffle bags. Two of them held bricks of cocaine, while the other held a quarter of a million dollars. He walked over to Monty and dropped all three bags at his feet, then sat back down.

"What's all this supposed to be?"

"It's what you came for, and it's what's going to get you where you need to be, shall you handle it right. I would give you more, but Montel gave me strict orders on the amount. If you fuck it up, that's on you, because you won't get anything else. Now, since we're done here, you can see yourself out."

Peanut got up and left the room again, but after about ten minutes, didn't return. So Monty grabbed the bags and went back up the stairs to the main floor. When he realized that he was by himself, he quickly walked out of the house and got in his ride. It wasn't that he was paranoid, but he was careful.

On his drive home, Monty constantly checked his rearview mirror. He had been robbed more than once, so he didn't want to take any chances. Thankfully, he pulled into his driveway without any problems. He got out, but left the drugs and money inside the Navigator. Monty decided that maybe he should listen to what he was told for once, because he couldn't stand another loss.

When Monty walked into the bedroom of his house, Cara was already in bed. She lay on her back, asleep, with a thin sheet covering her. As bad as he wanted to wake her and put some dick in her life, he wouldn't do it, because he was tired too.

Monty lay down and thought about his next move. He decided that the next day, he would go to ReLay's house and cook up some product. He would also go and talk to the company that Chance had bought his restaurant from to see if he could take it off their hands. Whatever Chance still owed, Monty would pay it. He had to do something to give back to him after all that Chance had done for him. He just hoped that nothing else stood in his way.

Chapter 15

"So you saying that you went to the prison and asked your father for help, after you've already been robbed of the other stuff he left you? Bruh, that right there took some guts."

"Now come on, ReLay, what the hell else was I supposed to do? My pops hears about everything that goes on out here, so sooner or later, someone would've told him about the stash getting jacked. I thought it would be best if he heard it from me."

"Yeah, I guess you right about that."

Monty had got up early and drove over to ReLay's house so he could help him cook up his product. Monty wanted to be on the block by sundown, and he knew that with ReLay's help, he would make it. It was Friday, and mufuckas would be out, swinging through the hood with their paychecks already cashed and ready to spend on their high. Monty wasn't trying to miss one dollar.

He had called the Realtor about the restaurant on his way to ReLay's, and they told him that Chance paid in full for the establishment. Upon his passing, the deed had been handed over to Thomas Hardy, known to Monty as Uncle Taboo. After they mentioned his uncle's name, Monty realized that he hadn't spoken to him since the day of Chance's funeral. He decided to make it his business and go see him before he hit the block that night.

ReLay lit a fat blunt and leaned back. Ever since Monty turned him onto the weed, he had been hooked. He liked how it mellowed him out, and most of all, now it kept his dick hard for hours and he couldn't wait to tell Monty about it.

"Nigga, I got to thank you. Ever since you turned me onto this shit, my dick stays hard, and now Zena got a whole new attitude. She be sweating my nut sack harder than a mufucka."

"Come on, Lay. Didn't I tell you that I don't want to hear about your dick? You can save that gay ass shit for Smash. Matter of fact, let me make a run over to my uncle's while you finish up here. Be ready to hit the block when I get back. Oh yeah, make sure you put some to the side for Darryl. I told him I was gone swing through with the re-up."

"A'ight, I can handle all that, but hurry up and get your ass back here. I'm ready to hit the block."

Monty walked out and left ReLay to handle the rest of the cocaine. He wasn't worried about his product because he knew that ReLay was dependable. ReLay had never given Monty a reason to question anything he did, and he hoped he never had to.

The drive to Taboo's felt like it took forever, although it was only a fifteen-minute ride. Monty charged it to his nervousness because he knew he should have been to see him sooner.

Taboo was sitting on the front porch of his house when Monty pulled up. To see him so alone made Monty feel even worse since he hadn't been around to check on him. Monty told himself that he would make it his business to stop by more often, especially since Chance was gone and Monty was now all he had.

"Unc, what's going on? I figured I needed to stop over and see how you been getting along."

"I been good, nephew. Just been here wondering if I was gone ever see you again. Didn't figure you had a reason to come by anymore. I did hear you went and saw Montel. That's good."

"Yeah, figured I'd listen for once and went on up there. It actually went better than I thought it would. Couldn't stay mad at him forever, ya know."

"No, Montana, you can't. You gotta believe that he didn't want to leave you and ya momma, and even though he did, it wasn't on his own free will. You got to forgive him and move on."

"I understand that now. That bitter feeling was eating me up inside, but I'm better now. I'm not here to talk about him, though. I actually came by to talk to you about the restaurant. I called the Realtor that Chance had went through and was told that the keys and the deed had been given to you."

"Yeah, I got all that. They said he had me listed as his beneficiary. But I don't know what I'ma do with it. Why do you ask?"

"Well, I'd like to buy it from you. I think it would only be right to keep it in the family. It would also be a way to keep my brother's dream alive. Ya know, a way to honor him."

"I don't know about all that now, because I know what you do out in them streets, and it would be disrespectful to dabble with that in the place. Chance had given up them streets, and I can't let you take them inside of what he had worked so hard for. Besides, I'd hate to worry about what happened to Chance, also happen to you. Montel would never forgive me."

"I understand, but something could happen whether I'm there or not. Can't dwell on that, though."

"You're right, and maybe you should think about that. Your brother and your friend are both six feet beneath the dirt, and your father has been locked up the majority of your life. You'll end up in one of those places if you don't change the things you out there doing. And as long as you in them streets, I can't give you them keys. Chance wouldn't have wanted that."

"How about we make a deal? You sell me the restaurant and give me six months, just to establish myself, and I give you my word that at the end of those six months, I'll go legit and get out of the streets."

"Oh really? So you're gonna turn in your gangsta card just like that? I'll believe it when I see it."

"I mean it. I'll give it all up. By then, the restaurant should be doing pretty well, and I'll still be able to pay my bills."

"Montana, with all due respect, as long as you have been out there in those gutters, you shouldn't have any bills. Everything you have should be owned, and what happened to what Montel had stored up for you? That should have been enough to sit you down."

"Let's just say that somebody else beat me to it and we'll leave it at that. But I want you to know that I'm gone get it together. I'm a make a nice future for me and Cara. Just give me a chance, Unc. A'ight?"

Taboo sat and thought about what Monty had proposed. He ultimately decided that he'd rather sell the restaurant to family than anybody else, and as long as Monty kept his word, Taboo knew it would be in good hands.

"Okay, Montana. I'ma let you get it, and I trust that in those six months, you won't disappoint me."

"I give you my word, Unc. I'm a make you, Chance, and my father proud. Just wait and see."

Monty hated to lie to Taboo, but he felt that at that moment he had no other choice. He figured it would be the only way to get him to agree to the sale. He couldn't believe how his uncle asked him to pull back from the streets, when he was the one who first put him out there. The streets was Monty's life, and once he went gangsta, he knew there would be no turning back.

After Monty had the keys and the deed to the restaurant, he passed his uncle seventy-five grand and then went on his way. Monty couldn't wait to get the place cleaned up and ready to run. He planned to have a special room built just for his product so he could have it stashed away safely.

On the way back to ReLay's house, Monty decided to stop and look inside the restaurant. Surprisingly, the door was unlocked. He figured that the police left it that way after they investigated the crime scene, so he brushed it off and went inside.

The scene before Monty brought tears to his eyes. The blood stains on the floor and wall made Monty wonder if Chance had suffered for long or if it was an instant death. He wondered just how Chance felt in those last moments of his life, and then he became angry. He wasn't going to stop until he figured out who ordered the hit on his brother. Rocky had only given him a small clue, and he had yet to find her.

Suddenly, Monty heard footsteps behind him and reached for his burner. Whoever it was would learn a quick lesson about walking up on him. Thankfully, before he turned around and fired, he heard Cara's voice.

"Your uncle told me I'd find you here. He thought I should come check on you. Are you okay?"

Monty placed his gun back in the waist of his jeans before he turned to face her. He should have known that Taboo would call her, at least for support, and Monty was glad he did.

"Baby, you don't have to worry about me. I'm good. I just wanted to stop by and check the place out. See how much cleaning up needs to be done."

"I figured as much. Your uncle told me you bought the place from him. Are you sure that's what you want to do?"

"Damn right, it is, and I was gonna run it by you myself, but when Unc agreed to sell it to me, I swiped it up. I didn't think you'd mind. I got to inspect the damage, see how much needs to be repaired, and most importantly, get it cleaned up. Can't do it right now, though. I got ReLay waiting on me about some business."

"Well, how about you go and meet up with ReLay and I'll stay here, look around, do a little cleaning, and make a list of what needs to be redone. I'm not doing anything else today anyway."

"Hell nah. I'm not about to let you stay up in here by yourself. Not after what happened to my brother."

"Come on, Monty, I'll be fine. Besides, it might be a little too much, too soon for you. Let me help."

Monty thought about it for a minute. He did appreciate her offering to help, and she would be the perfect person to take care of what needed to be done.

"If I agree to let you do this, you got to promise to keep the doors locked and the alarm needs to be on. You also have to call me as soon as you get ready to leave."

"Okay, daddy. I will do just as you say. Now go and do what you need to do. I'll see you at home."

Monty made sure Cara locked the door like he'd asked. He knew he would lose his mind if something happened to her, so he went and called Smash to sit across the street and watch over her. Monty felt better knowing that someone was there to keep her safe. When he made it back to ReLay's, he told him all that had transpired with Taboo, and with Cara. ReLay couldn't believe that Monty actually left her there by herself, so he decided to ask him about it.

"Aye, Monty, you ain't worried about ya girl being up in that place by herself after what happened?"

"Of course I am, that's why I called Smash. He's sitting outside keeping an eye on things. I think it's all for nothing, though. I mean, the bitch who put the hit out on Chance has to know a mufucka is looking for her. She'd be a fool to make another move."

"Well, she may not know that Rocky snitched her out like that, but I guess since Smash is there, ya girl should be good. He ain't gone let a mufucka get close at all."

"I know, and that's why I called him. Now come on and let's hit the block. You already know that them fiends ain't gone wait too long. I don't want to miss out."

Monty and ReLay went out on the block and posted up. By the end of the night, they had sold every piece of dope they brought with them. Monty was certain that if they would have brought more, it would have sold out too.

"Damn, Monty. We straight up did that shit. Them mufuckin' fiends was going crazy. You know what, though? I been meaning to ask you. You got all those bricks that you could use for a quicker come up by supplying them to the niggas who need a plug, and yet, you choose to cook that shit up and then come out here on the block to push dimes and twenties. What the hell is up with that? Wouldn't you make more in the long run if you did it the other way?"

"Ya know, Lay? That's a good ass question, and I do have an answer for you. This street shit makes my dick hard. I live for this. I like to be on the scene, so I can't imagine sitting my ass at home and waiting for a mufucka to need a re-up on they supply. Ya know what I mean?"

"I guess, but I know a nigga right now that would take ten of them bricks off your hand. It wouldn't even put a dent in what you went and picked up."

"You know a nigga, huh? So you been trying to work deals behind my back?"

"Hell nah, I would never try you like that. It's just, my cousin called from New Orleans and said her boyfriend was looking for a plug. Said he's even willing to pay up to twenty-six a brick. Nigga, that's two hundred sixty grand. You could take that and buy twice what you gave up. I'm just thinking about the long-term investment in this. Ain't that what you pay me for?"

Monty thought about it. ReLay was right, and the flip would make him more in the end. Monty was almost certain that Peanut would give him a good deal if he came with that gwop, and because of that, Monty agreed.

"A'ight, I'm a go head and trust you on this, but ain't nothing being given on consignment. Ya feel me?"

"Consignment, shit, Darius don't even play like that. He always gives his money at delivery. My cousin wouldn't have called me with that type of play, anyway."

"Well, how do you know what he does in the first place? You done dealt with him before?"

"Nah, not on that tip, but when I would go and spend the summer out there, he was making big moves. I don't know what happened to his plug, though. All I know is that he needs a new one."

Monty decided that he would go ahead and let ReLay set the buy up, and take the trip to New Orleans himself. Hell, he needed a vacation, and he would make sure the trip wasn't only for business. Monty was going to have a little fun too.

"A'ight, Lay. You ain't never led me wrong before, so go head and call him up and tell him we coming out. I'm telling you now though, if something goes wrong, you gone pay for it."

"I ain't even worried about it, because Darius is good people. I wouldn't put you on to him if he wasn't. I can tell you this, you gone be glad you fucked with him."

"For your sake, I better be."

ReLay just smiled and nodded. He was happy that Monty trusted him and would never do anything to change that. Monty had given him a chance when no one else would, so ReLay felt like he would forever owe him nothing but his loyalty. ReLay would kill, steal, and even die for Monty. He just hoped it never came to that. If it did, he would be ready to take one for the team.

"Say, boss, you gone take ya girl on the trip?"

"Hell nah. I hear that New Orleans pussy is where it's at. How I'ma find out if it's true if Cara's beside me? Why you ask that? You trying to take Zena?"

"Nawl, bruh. I'm trying to run up in something new. I was just trying to make sure that we on the same page."

Monty laughed, because honestly, ReLay thought a lot like him, and he was cool with that. Monty took ReLay back home and went his own way. He wasn't sure how Cara would feel about him leaving town for a few days, but he was doing it whether she liked it or not.

Monty was on a new come-up mission, one that he planned to execute successfully. He was tired of mufuckas feeling like they could take what he'd worked so hard for. From that day on, Monty was in it to win it. However, there would always be someone who wouldn't want him to make it to the finish line.

Chapter 16

Monty pulled Cara close and then leaned down to kiss her. The way her tongue intertwined with his made him want to fuck her right there, but he had ReLay waiting on him, so the pussy would have to wait—at least until he got to his destination.

"So tell me, baby. What you gone do while I'm gone?"

"Come on, Monty. You act like you're going to be gone a long time, when you and I both know you can't stay away from me for that long."

"You damn right, I can't. I just don't want you to get too bored without me here and find another nigga to fill that time."

"You're real funny, and you know that's not going to happen. I'm actually going to be busy trying to finish up what needs to be done at the restaurant. I know you're ready to get it open and keep your brother's dream alive."

"Yeah, about that. I think at the re-opening ceremony we should have some kind of tribute for him, just so no one forgets who started it all."

"That sounds great, and I think he would like it very much. Chance would be so proud of all you're doing, and I'm proud too."

Monty felt his cell phone vibrate and pulled it from his back pocket. He read the text from ReLay that let him know he was ready to go. Monty showed the text to Cara, who only smiled in turn. She had never revealed her true feelings to Monty, but she didn't care for ReLay—no matter how much her man bragged about him.

"That's an impatient ass nigga right there, but I do got to get out of here. I'll call you when I get there."

Monty picked up his bag and walked out. He was lucky to have a woman like Cara that he could leave for days at a time and know that she would still be there when he got back. Plus, she respected him, and that meant more than anything.

When Monty pulled up to ReLay's, he was on the front porch steps talking on the phone, but as soon as he saw Monty, he ended the call.

"Man, that bitch is nagging the hell out of me. Lord knows I need this time away, because Zena been tripping ever since I told her. For some reason, she can't comprehend that she ain't coming. Stupid bitch packed a bag and all."

"That's just what your ass gets. You say you be smoking a blunt and then putting it down, but you doing too much. You got to start holding back a little, you know—keep her wondering if it gets better each time. Stop giving Zena all the dick at once. Make her ass wait on it."

"Now how am I supposed to do that when she make the pussy so damn good?"

"And yet, you 'bout to hit the streets of New Orleans looking for something new to run up in."

"Yeah, that may be true, but at the end of the day, I'm a always go home to Zena."

Monty shook his head and then pushed in a *Tank* CD. ReLay cut his eyes at him but knew better than to say anything. Instead, he pulled out a small baggie of weed and a *Swisher Sweet*. He was about to split the cigar open, but Monty stopped him.

"The fuck is wrong with you, nigga? We riding down the interstate dirty and you gone smoke a blunt? What if I get pulled over? One smell of that shit will have us in the back of the police car while they tear this shit up. At least if I do get stopped and they don't smell nothing, I stand a better chance. So put that shit away."

"Damn, bruh. I'm just trying to relax a little. You done put in that lame-ass disc, at least let me do something that'll help me block it out."

Monty looked over at ReLay and then ejected the Tank CD. He put a *Jackboy* disc in its place and turned the volume up. ReLay smiled and began to bob his head to the beat. A few hours later, Monty crossed into the New Orleans city limits.

"Oh shit, we here, boss. Let me hit my cousin up and tell her we'll be there in about ten minutes."

"We ain't gone be nowhere if you don't tell me where to go."

"Oh, my bad."

ReLay told Monty how to get to his cousin Nisha's house and then called to let her know they were about to pull up. Nisha's mother and ReLay's father were brother and sister and raised the two of them close to each other. Nisha was only two years older than him, and a little wiser when it came to the streets—but only because she had a dope-boy fetish.

When Monty pulled up to the house ReLay had given him directions to, the first thing he noticed was the yellow-bone honey standing on the front porch. He really didn't do light-skinned bitches because they were known to have stank-ass attitudes, but the one he had his eyes on could be the exception.

"Dayum! Who in the hell is that fine-ass female on the porch? And don't tell me that's *our* cousin, because I might fire your ass."

"Yep, that's Nisha, and if I know her like I think I do, you just her type—but remember, it's her nigga Darius that we came to see."

"Yeah, but he ain't part of my crew, so he don't count."

"But Monty, you know the same rules apply, so tread lightly and let's get his money."

Monty shook his head because, one, he couldn't believe that ReLay had never introduced him to his cousin, and two, now that he would meet her, wasn't shit he could do. He wanted to say, *fuck the code of the streets*, but that would only cause drama he didn't need.

ReLay stepped out of the Navigator with Monty close behind. He walked up on the porch, hugged Nisha, and then introduced her to his boss.

"Sup, cuz? This here is Monty—the only mufucka who was willing to give me a chance in the game, and the one I told you about to help Darius."

Nisha smiled and looked Monty up and down. His starched-up *Tommy Hilfiger* jeans and white tee made her insides flutter. She glanced down at his clean white *Timbs* and raised her eyebrows. Nisha walked up close to him and ran her fingers over the diamond-encrusted king cobra charm that hung from the platinum chain around his neck.

"This real, or you wear it just for show like so many others who proclaim to be a gangsta?"

Monty gave her a serious look and then pushed her hand away. As much as he would have liked to fuck her, he knew he couldn't, so he didn't want to give her the wrong idea.

"I ain't never proclaimed to be anything but me, and everything I do, say, and wear is the real deal. I don't know what you used to, but this ain't where it's at, so I'll ask that you respect my boundaries and I'll do the same."

About that time, a brown-skinned brother covered in tattoos on his chest and arms walked out on the front porch. He nodded at ReLay and then motioned for Nisha to go inside before he turned to Monty and spoke.

"Don't mind her. She try every mufucka that comes my way, but you the first one to pass the test. That alone tells me that you gone keep shit between us one hundred at all times, and that is a good thing. I'm Darius, by the way."

Darius held out his hand for Monty to shake and then invited him and ReLay inside. Thankfully, Nisha was nowhere to be seen, because Monty wasn't sure he could ignore her fat ass and thick thighs. Plus, he would hate for

Darius to catch him looking and think that he was a sneaky mufucka.

The inside of the house was immaculate. Monty was almost certain that someone other than Nisha kept it clean—'cause even though she looked like a good fuck, she didn't strike him as the house-wife type. She was too hood, and her manicure said she didn't even do dishes. That almost turned Monty off . . . almost.

"This a nice place you got here."

"Yeah, thanks. Sad to say, but my auntie comes by once a week and gives it a good clean-up. If it wasn't for her, this place would probably be a wreck. I'm mostly always in the streets, and Nisha either at the hairdresser, the nail salon, or somewhere shopping with her messy-ass girlfriends."

"Well, I guess I'm grateful to have a woman who don't mind taking care of things."

"Well, you a lucky mufucka, so make sure you hold on to her. Don't get me wrong, I love my bitch, but she a hood rat to the extreme."

All three men laughed at the comment and then got down to business. ReLay started the conversation to make things more comfortable.

"So, Darius, I told my boy here what you was looking for, and he straight on that, but I'ma go in here to the kitchen and find me a snack while the two of you talk about it. I'll be back."

As soon as ReLay left the living room, Darius turned to Monty. He had been without a plug for months and was anxious to get started with something new.

"So, Monty, first of all, I appreciate you coming all this way to handle this. ReLay tells me you got what I'm looking for, and I'm ready to deal."

"That ain't no problem, but I'm curious—what happened to your other plug?"

"That's a fair question, and I can answer that very easily. My old connect, Mando—well, he got drunk one night and ran himself into a light pole. I tried to find a way to hook up with his people, but they refused to deal with an American. So here I am, trying to establish ties elsewhere."

"ReLay said you wanted ten, so that's all I brought—but just so you know up front, I don't do consignment."

"And I would never ask you to. I'm a businessman, and I deal only with businessmen. Don't let these tattoos fool you—I don't hang in the hood on a street corner and wait for juggs to come ask me for a hit. That's not my steelo. I only deal with mufuckas who, in the end, I can benefit from. Doctors, lawyers, even some politicians. People mistake me for a corner boy all the time, and that's how I want to keep it—but I don't wear drops and Timbs. I wear suits and loafers. Don't get me wrong, I used to be out there, but a wise old man scooped me up and taught me how to be a better dealer. I don't have time to go out and pull guns on mufuckas about what they owe me. That's why I deal with who I deal with—and to keep them happy, I give them their money's worth."

"Enough said, and I got to commend you on that, but my forte is the streets. That's where I get my joy from. However, I do respect the fact that you do things different. Who knows? Maybe one day, I'll get tired of serving the fiends and move up to professionals. We'll see."

"Ain't nothing wrong with being out there on the block. I get it, and I respect it. Now, if we could get down to business and get it done, perhaps I could give you a tour of the city."

"A'ight. My plan was to give you those ten birds for twenty-eight each, but I like your style and I feel like this is going to be the start of a lucrative, respectable relationship. So, I'm going to give them to you for twenty-five instead."

"That number sounds wonderful, and you'll get paid in full. Stay loaded though, because I'ma be a repeat customer, and my people, they will be forever grateful if I don't run out."

"Speaking of your people, you wouldn't happen to have any federal judges in your pockets, would you?"

"Why do you ask? You got a federal case going on or something?"

"Nah, not me, but my father does. He's been locked up in the feds since I was five years old. Killed a crooked agent who ran a mock raid on him. The agent killed his best friend in the process, so my father got revenge."

"Tell you what. I'll talk to someone and see if they can look into it, and then we'll go from there. How's that sound?"

"Sounds better than what I could have expected. Now let's go ahead and handle what I came here for, 'cause I'm ready to go out and explore what New Orleans has to offer."

After Monty and Darius handled their business, they hit the town. Everywhere they went, Monty took notice of how well-respected Darius was. It seemed as if men and women alike wanted to be in his presence. Monty hoped to one day be on that same status. He already had hood celebrity, but to have it on a business level would mean even more.

The guys had been out for over an hour when Darius had to cut his night short. He had clients he needed to go and see the next day and wanted to get a good night's sleep. It was also getting late, and he knew Nisha would be tripping, and he didn't feel like hearing her mouth.

"Alright, fellas, I'ma have to cut it short here, but I'll get back up with you before you leave. And Monty, you make sure you have a good time. I want you to have more than one reason to come back."

"Oh, I can assure you, I'm gone have a great time as soon as I lay my eyes on the right female."

Darius laughed and then left Monty and ReLay to themselves. They decided to hit the nearest strip club so they could see how the New Orleans dancers moved. When the dancers found out they were out of town, they put extra pep in their step. They knew that the out-of-towners paid better than the locals, and they weren't about to miss out.

ReLay had a dark-skinned dancer in a peach thong grinding on his lap. Her fat ass jiggled like a bowl of jello and had him on swole, while Monty had a short white girl with big titties grinding on him.

"Damn, Lay. These New Orleans ho's ratchet as a mufucka. I say we go ahead and get outta here so they can really grind on some dick."

"Shiiit, I'm all the way with you on that. Let's go."

After a promise of good pay, the two women left the club with Monty and ReLay. They had already secured hotel rooms before hitting the town, specifically for that purpose. However, in the middle of getting his dick sucked by the white girl, Monty felt guilty and had a change of heart.

"Hey, yo. I don't think I'm gone be able to do this and then go home and look my woman in the face."

The white girl stopped giving him head and looked up at him. Never in her life had a man not wanted her to finish. She was pissed. Not because he stopped her, but because she knew she would not be getting the dick.

"What do you mean you can't do this? Don't you think it's a little too late to feel guilty? I mean, you've gone this far, you might as well finish."

"Nah, lil' mama, that ain't gone happen. Go ahead and get dressed. I'ma give you a little extra money so you can catch a cab back."

Monty immediately picked up his phone and called her a cab. He could tell that she tried to stall in hopes that he would change his mind, but little did she know, it wasn't going to happen. When the cab pulled up, he opened the door for her so she could see how serious he really was.

The next morning, ReLay couldn't believe his ears when Monty told him what happened, because he didn't think any man in their right mind would turn down some pussy.

"So, you mean to tell me that you stopped the bitch from giving you head and told her never mind?"

"Well, she had already started, but I cut that shit short. I don't know, Lay, it's like I kept seeing Cara's face and felt guilty as a mufucka."

"Well, that's your loss, 'cause I had that real chocolaty bitch in every position I could think of. Even some I made up. Pussy was juicy too. I'ma find that bitch next time we come back too."

That afternoon, Monty and ReLay went ahead and left New Orleans. Monty told himself that when he went back, he would take Cara too, so that way, he wouldn't feel so bad.

Chapter 17

After Monty dropped ReLay off at home, he took a quick drive through the block, just to see if anything was going on. When he saw only a few fiends out, he pushed on and stopped by Darryl's to check out things on his end.

"What's up, Darryl? I was on my way home and figured I'd stop by, see how shit is going with the product."

"Ah man, I'm almost out. Them fiends went crazy for it. I would ask for a re-up, but I know you got more important things to deal with right now."

"The fuck you mean by that?"

"I mean that place Chance had up and running before he was ambushed. It burnt down last night. Don't tell me you ain't heard."

"You got to be mistaken. Cara would've called me immediately if something like that happened."

"Well, I don't know why she didn't, because it did happen. Shit been all over the news. That place was destroyed."

Monty didn't want to believe what Darryl had told him, so as soon as he left him, he went to see for himself. Sure enough, when he pulled up, there was nothing left but piles of burnt-up rubbish. Monty could still see smoke rising from the debris and wondered why Cara hadn't contacted him—especially since it was something he needed to know about. His chest tightened, anger crawling up his throat as the smell of burnt wood and ashes hit him. That was his brother's dream, gone in smoke, and for the first time in a long time, Monty felt powerless.

He drove away and rushed home so he could find out just what the hell was going on. When he pulled up in the driveway, Cara was already outside on the porch, as if she knew he'd be there.

"I'm so sorry, Monty. I know I should've called, but I didn't want to ruin what you had going on."

"The fuck you mean? Don't you think that was important enough to give me a call? How the hell did it happen?"

"I don't know how it happened, and I won't know anything until the fire investigator gets done with what he needs to do. Thanks for asking if I'm okay, though."

"Sorry, baby. I just . . . damn, every time I feel like I'm about to get ahead, something else pushes me back. I don't fuckin' understand."

"It's okay, Monty. We can rebuild or even find another place. We'll be okay."

"Rebuild? How the hell I'm a do that when I'm barely standin' myself?"

"We will get through this, just like everything else."

Monty looked at Cara and, without saying a word, turned around and went back to his ride. He had too much shit running through his mind all at once and needed some time alone to sort it out. First, though, he had to go check on his uncle, because Monty could no longer keep the promise he made him.

The lights inside Taboo's house were off when Monty pulled up, but he could see the flicker of the television screen, so he got out and knocked. A few minutes later, Taboo opened the door and invited him inside.

"What took you so long? I been waitin' on you all day, but you don't have to explain anything to me. These kinds of things happen all the time."

"Sorry, Unc, but I was out of town, and I just found out. I would've been here immediately had I known."

"Well, like I said, you don't owe me an explanation. What you need to do is start payin' attention to your surroundings and the people who share it. You got an enemy, Montana, and I think they're closer than you know."

"Why you say that, Unc? I wasn't even there when it happened."

"You may not have been there, but somebody had to know of your plans, and they stopped you. I know your father told you to keep your business to yourself, and you need to listen to him before you end up like your brother. I don't wanna see that happen."

"Oh, don't worry about me. I'm always careful, and I keep that four-five and the AR ready."

"Those guns don't mean anything when you're around people you think you can trust. They're the ones you got to keep an eye on."

Monty caught on to what Taboo was trying to tell him and decided that maybe he should be more cautious—at least until he found out who put the hit on Chance. He felt like he should talk to Cara again about the night he was shot, since her and ReLay had two different versions.

"Thanks for the advice, and I'ma take heed. But right now, I need to get back home and talk to Cara about somethin' I been meanin' to bring up for a minute now. Maybe then I'll have a little insight to everything."

"Alright, Montana. Just be careful out there."

Monty drove straight back home so he could get some answers only Cara could give him about the night he and Dreybo got shot. Thankfully, when he walked into the bedroom, she was still awake.

"Oh my gosh, Monty. Where the hell did you go? I been so worried. Are you okay?"

Cara got out of bed and wrapped her arms around his neck while he gripped her small waist. Other than ReLay, she was the only person he had told about his plans for the restaurant, and since Monty knew that Cara was solid, he had to wonder if ReLay still was.

"Baby, I need to talk to you about the night me and Drey were shot."

"Okay, Monty. Go ahead."

"I need to know if me and him were the only two who were shot at that night."

"I thought I already told you that there were several others, but your friend was the only one besides the dancer he was with that didn't make it out. Why are you bringing that up?"

"Because ReLay tellin' me different. He's tryin' to make me believe it was a hit. I need to know the truth, 'cause if I got an enemy out there, I need to know."

"Oh, Monty, don't let him put things in your head like that. Aren't you wonderin' why he'd tell you that all of a sudden? Have you questioned his motive?"

"Nah, didn't think I had to. But so much shit's happenin', and other than you, he's the only one who knows my business."

"Well, why don't you worry about that another time? You had a long trip, and ya girl missed you."

"Oh, really?"

"Yes, baby. I missed you really bad. Come on and let me show you how much."

Monty followed Cara to the bed and stripped. He was exhausted—not only from the ride back from New Orleans, but from everything else going on too. However, he was never too tired to please his woman, so before he closed his eyes, he gave her what she had missed.

Monty lay in the bed and thought about ReLay until he fell asleep. He found it hard to believe that his protégé would betray him like that, but Monty was all out of other options. He would make it his business to confront him the next day about everything.

The next morning, when Monty got up, he showered and got dressed. After he laced up his *Air Force 1s*, he pulled the four-five out of his drawer and tucked it in the waist of his jeans. He turned back and looked at Cara, who slept as if she had no worries—something Monty wished he could do, but that would have to wait.

Monty leaned over and kissed Cara on the forehead, then walked out of the room. He went downstairs and grabbed a bagel before he walked out of the house. He was hungry as a mufucka, but the bagel would have to do. When Monty got in his Navigator and pushed the key in the ignition, he felt his cell phone vibrate. He thought it might've been ReLay trying to get an early start, so he answered on the first ring.

When he answered, he heard the automated voice that came through when his father called. It was strange for him to call so early, but Monty accepted the call anyway.

He pressed nine on the phone pad so the call could go through, but before he even had a chance to say hello, Montel had something to say.

"I need you to come see me as soon as possible. I remember where I know her from."

To Be Continued

Coming Soon:
***Once You Go Gangsta* Part 2:**
Glocks & Roses

Lock Down Publications and Ca$h Presents
Assisted Publishing Packages

Due to an increase in the price of services we have increased our prices. The prices below reflect the price increase as of 11/1/24.

BASIC PACKAGE	UPGRADED PACKAGE
$699	**$1000**
Editing	Typing
Cover Design	Editing
Formatting	Cover Design
	Formatting
	Upload eBooks to Amazon
	Upload Paperback to Amazon
ADVANCE PACKAGE	**LDP SUPREME PACKAGE**
$1,400	**$1,700**
Typing	Typing
Editing (line editing/content)	Editing (line editing/content)
Cover Design	Cover Design
Formatting	Formatting
Copyright Registration	Copyright Registration
Proofreading	Proofreading
Upload eBooks to Amazon	Set up Amazon Account
Upload Paperback to Amazon	Upload eBooks to Amazon
	Upload Paperback to Amazon
	Advertise on LDP's Amazon and
	Facebook Page

***

Other services available upon request.
Additional charges may apply

Lock Down Publications
P.O. Box 944
Stockbridge, GA 30281-9998
Phone: 470 303-9761
Email: lockdownpublications@gmail.com

Submission Guideline

Submit the first three chapters of your completed manuscript to ldpsubmissions@gmail.com. In the subject line add **Your Book's Title**. The manuscript must be in a Word Doc file and sent as an attachment. Document should be in Times New Roman, double spaced, and in size 12 font. Also, provide your synopsis and full contact information. If sending multiple submissions, they must each be in a separate email.

Have a story but no way to send it electronically? You can still submit to LDP/Ca$h Presents. Send in the first three chapters, written or typed, of your completed manuscript to:

LDP: Submissions Dept
P.O. Box 944
Stockbridge, GA 30281-9998

DO NOT send original manuscript. Must be a duplicate. Provide your synopsis and a cover letter containing your full contact information.

Thanks for considering LDP and Ca$h Presents.

NEW RELEASES

BLOODLINE OF A SAVAGE 1-3
THESE VICIOUS STREETS 1-3

RELENTLESS GOON 1-3
BY PRINCE A. TAUHID

THE BUTTERFLY MAFIA 1-3
BY FUMIYA PAYNE

A THUG'S STREET PRINCESS 1&2
BY MEESHA

CITY OF SMOKE 3
BY MOLOTTI

GET IT IN SLUGS 1 &2
BY B. STALL

STANDING ON HER BUSINESS 1&2
BY DG SANTANA

STEPPERS 1,2&3
THE REAL BADDIES OF CHI-RAQ
BY KING RIO

THE LANE 1&2
BY KEN-KEN SPENCE

THUG OF SPADES 1&2
LOVE IN THE TRENCHES 2
CORNER BOYS
BY COREY ROBINSON

TIL DEATH 3
BY ARYANNA

THE BIRTH OF A GANGSTER 4
BY DELMONT PLAYER

PRODUCT OF THE STREETS 1-3
BY DEMOND "MONEY" ANDERSON

NO TIME FOR ERROR
BY KEESE

MONEY HUNGRY DEMONS 1-2
BY TRANAY ADAMS

HUB CITY MENACE 1-3
BY J. WHITE

A THUGGISH PASSION 1&2
LAND OF DA HOOLIGANZ 1-4
KILLAZ ON STANDBY 1&2
BY IRA B.

FO'EVA ROLLIN 1&2
BY ASSA RAYMOND BAKER

THE LEVEL UP 1&3
BY LUXURY KING

**Coming Soon from Lock Down
Publications/Ca$h Presents**

IF YOU CROSS ME ONCE 6
ANGEL V
By Anthony Fields

A THUGS STREET PRINCESS 3
By Meesha

CORNER BOYS 2
By Corey Robinson

THA TAKEOVER
By Keith Chandler

BETRAYAL OF A G 2
By Ray Vinci

SAVAGE FAMILY EMPIRE 1&2
SOULLESS GOON 1,2&3
THE DIRTY SIDE OF MONEY 1,2&3
By Prince

FOR MY ENEMY'S SAKE
AMBITIONS OF A SLIDER
FRESH OFF DA PORCH
By IRA B.

BY THE TRUCKLOAD 1-4
TIPPIN' THE SCALES 1-3
BAD BITCHES WIT GUNZ 3
PROBLEM SOLVED 2
By Christopher "Diesel" Hornezes

Available Now

RESTRAINING ORDER 1 & 2
By **CA$H & Coffee**

LOVE KNOWS NO BOUNDARIES 1-3
By **Coffee**

RAISED AS A GOON I, II, III & IV
BRED BY THE SLUMS I, II, III
BLAST FOR ME I & II
ROTTEN TO THE CORE I II III
A BRONX TALE I, II, III
DUFFLE BAG CARTEL I II III IV V VI
HEARTLESS GOON I II III IV V
A SAVAGE DOPEBOY I II
DRUG LORDS I II III
CUTTHROAT MAFIA I II
KING OF THE TRENCHES
By **Ghost**

LAY IT DOWN I & II
LAST OF A DYING BREED I II
BLOOD STAINS OF A SHOTTA I & II III
By **Jamaica**

LOYAL TO THE GAME I II III
LIFE OF SIN I, II III
By **TJ & Jelissa**

IF LOVING HIM IS WRONG…I & II
LOVE ME EVEN WHEN IT HURTS I II III
By **Jelissa**

PUSH IT TO THE LIMIT
By **Bre' Hayes**

BLOODY COMMAS I & II
SKI MASK CARTEL I, II & III
KING OF NEW YORK I II, III IV V
RISE TO POWER I II III
COKE KINGS I II III IV V

BORN HEARTLESS I II III IV
KING OF THE TRAP I II
By **T.J. Edwards**

WHEN THE STREETS CLAP BACK I & II III
THE HEART OF A SAVAGE I II III IV
MONEY MAFIA I II
LOYAL TO THE SOIL I II III
By **Jibril Williams**

A DISTINGUISHED THUG STOLE MY HEART I II & III
LOVE SHOULDN'T HURT I II III IV
RENEGADE BOYS 1-4
PAID IN KARMA 1-3
SAVAGE STORMS 1-3
AN UNFORESEEN LOVE 1-3
BABY, I'M WINTERTIME COLD 1-3
A THUG'S STREET PRINCESS 1&2
By **Meesha**

A GANGSTER'S CODE 1-3
A GANGSTER'S SYN 1-3
THE SAVAGE LIFE 1-3
CHAINED TO THE STREETS 1-3
BLOOD ON THE MONEY 1-3
A GANGSTA'S PAIN 1-3
BEAUTIFUL LIES AND UGLY TRUTHS
CHURCH IN THESE STREETS
By **J-Blunt**

CUM FOR ME 1-8
An LDP Erotica Collaboration

BLOOD OF A BOSS 1-5
SHADOWS OF THE GAME
TRAP BASTARD
By **Askari**

ONCE YOU GO GANGSTA | COREY ROBINSON

THE STREETS BLEED MURDER 1-3
THE HEART OF A GANGSTA 1-3
By **Jerry Jackson**

WHEN A GOOD GIRL GOES BAD
By **Adrienne**

THE COST OF LOYALTY 1-3
By **Kweli**

BRIDE OF A HUSTLA 1-3
THE FETTI GIRLS 1-3
CORRUPTED BY A GANGSTA 1-4
BLINDED BY HIS LOVE
THE PRICE YOU PAY FOR LOVE 1-3
DOPE GIRL MAGIC 1-3
By **Destiny Skai**

A KINGPIN'S AMBITION
A KINGPIN'S AMBITION II
I MURDER FOR THE DOUGH
By **Ambitious**

TRUE SAVAGE 1-7
DOPE BOY MAGIC 1-3
MIDNIGHT CARTEL 1-3
CITY OF KINGZ 1&2
NIGHTMARE ON SILENT AVE
THE PLUG OF LIL MEXICO 1&2
CLASSIC CITY
By **Chris Green**

A GANGSTER'S REVENGE 1-4
THE BOSS MAN'S DAUGHTERS 1-5
A SAVAGE LOVE 1&2
BAE BELONGS TO ME 1&2
A HUSTLER'S DECEIT 1-3

WHAT BAD BITCHES DO 1-3
SOUL OF A MONSTER 1-3
KILL ZONE
A DOPE BOY'S QUEEN 1-3
TIL DEATH 1-3
IMMA DIE BOUT MINE 1-6
DYING FOR LIKES
By **Aryanna**

A DOPEBOY'S PRAYER
By **Eddie "Wolf" Lee**

THE KING CARTEL 1-3
By **Frank Gresham**

THESE NIGGAS AIN'T LOYAL 1-3
By **Nikki Tee**

GANGSTA SHYT 1-3
By **CATO**

THE ULTIMATE BETRAYAL
By **Phoenix**

BOSS'N UP 1-3
By **Royal Nicole**

I LOVE YOU TO DEATH
By **Destiny J**

I RIDE FOR MY HITTA
I STILL RIDE FOR MY HITTA
By **Misty Holt**

LOVE & CHASIN' PAPER
By **Qay Crockett**

TO DIE IN VAIN
SINS OF A HUSTLA

ONCE YOU GO GANGSTA | COREY ROBINSON
By **ASAD**

BROOKLYN HUSTLAZ
By **Boogsy Morina**

BROOKLYN ON LOCK 1 & 2
By **Sonovia**

GANGSTA CITY
By **Teddy Duke**

A DRUG KING AND HIS DIAMOND 1-3
A DOPEMAN'S RICHES
HER MAN, MINE'S TOO 1&2
CASH MONEY HO'S
THE WIFEY I USED TO BE 1&2
PRETTY GIRLS DO NASTY THINGS
By **Nicole Goosby**

LIPSTICK KILLAH 1-3
CRIME OF PASSION 1-3
FRIEND OR FOE 1-3
By **Mimi**

TRAPHOUSE KING 1-3
KINGPIN KILLAZ 1-3
STREET KINGS 1&2
PAID IN BLOOD 1&2
CARTEL KILLAZ 1-3
DOPE GODS 1&2
By **Hood Rich**

THE STREETS ARE CALLING
By **Duquie Wilson**

STEADY MOBBN' 1-3
THE STREETS STAINED MY SOUL 1-3
By **Marcellus Allen**

WHO SHOT YA 1-3
SON OF A DOPE FIEND 1-4
HEAVEN GOT A GHETTO 1&2
SKI MASK MONEY 1&2
By **Renta**

GORILLAZ IN THE BAY 1-4
TEARS OF A GANGSTA 1/&2
3X KRAZY 1&2
STRAIGHT BEAST MODE 1&2
By **DE'KARI**

TRIGGADALE 1-3
MURDA WAS THE CASE 1-3
By **Elijah R. Freeman**

SLAUGHTER GANG 1-3
RUTHLESS HEART 1-3
By **Willie Slaughter**

GOD BLESS THE TRAPPERS 1-3
THESE SCANDALOUS STREETS 1-3
FEAR MY GANGSTA 1-5
THESE STREETS DON'T LOVE NOBODY 1-2
BURY ME A G 1-5
A GANGSTA'S EMPIRE 1-4
THE DOPEMAN'S BODYGAURD 1&2
THE REALEST KILLAZ 1-3
THE LAST OF THE OGS 1-3
By **Tranay Adams**

MARRIED TO A BOSS 1-3
By **Destiny Skai & Chris Green**

KINGZ OF THE GAME 1-7
CRIME BOSS 1-4
By **Playa Ray**

FUK SHYT
By **Blakk Diamond**

DON'T F#CK WITH MY HEART 1&2
By **Linnea**

ADDICTED TO THE DRAMA 1-3
IN THE ARM OF HIS BOSS
By **Jamila**

LOYALTY AIN'T PROMISED 1&2
By **Keith Williams**

YAYO 1-4
A SHOOTER'S AMBITION 1&2
BRED IN THE GAME
By **S. Allen**

TRAP GOD 1-3
RICH $AVAGE 1-3
MONEY IN THE GRAVE 1-3
CARTEL MONEY 1&2
By **Martell Troublesome Bolden**

FOREVER GANGSTA 1&2
GLOCKS ON SATIN SHEETS 1&2
By **Adrian Dulan**

TOE TAGZ 1-4
LEVELS TO THIS SHYT 1&2
IT'S JUST ME AND YOU
By **Ah'Million**

KINGPIN DREAMS 1-3
RAN OFF ON DA PLUG
By **Paper Boi Rari**

THE STREETS MADE ME 1-3

By **Larry D. Wright**

CONFESSIONS OF A GANGSTA 1-4
CONFESSIONS OF A JACKBOY 1-3
CONFESSIONS OF A HITMAN
CONFESSIONS OF A DOPE BOY
By **Nicholas Lock**

I'M NOTHING WITHOUT HIS LOVE
SINS OF A THUG
TO THE THUG I LOVED BEFORE
A GANGSTA SAVED XMAS
IN A HUSTLER I TRUST
By **Monet Dragun**

QUIET MONEY 1-3
THUG LIFE 1-3
EXTENDED CLIP 1&2
A GANGSTA'S PARADISE
By **Trai'Quan**

CAUGHT UP IN THE LIFE 1-3
THE STREETS NEVER LET GO 1-3
By **Robert Baptiste**

NEW TO THE GAME 1-3
MONEY, MURDER & MEMORIES 1-3
By **Malik D. Rice**

CREAM 2-3
THE STREETS WILL TALK
By **Yolanda Moore**

THE STREETS WILL NEVER CLOSE 1-3
By **K'ajji**

LIFE OF A SAVAGE 1-4
A GANGSTA'S QUR'AN 1-4

MURDA SEASON 1-3
GANGLAND CARTEL 1-3
CHI'RAQ GANGSTAS 1-4
KILLERS ON ELM STREET 1-3
JACK BOYZ N DA BRONX 1-3
A DOPEBOY'S DREAM 1-3
JACK BOYS VS DOPE BOYS 1-3
COKE GIRLZ
COKE BOYS
SOSA GANG 1&2
BRONX SAVAGES
BODYMORE KINGPINS
BLOOD OF A GOON
By **Romell Tukes**

CONCRETE KILLA 1-3
VICIOUS LOYALTY 1-3
BLOODY MONEY BAGS
By **Kingpen**

THE ULTIMATE SACRIFICE 1-6
KHADIFI
IF YOU CROSS ME ONCE 1-3
ANGEL 1-4
IN THE BLINK OF AN EYE
By **Anthony Fields**

THE LIFE OF A HOOD STAR
By **Ca$h & Rashia Wilson**

NIGHTMARES OF A HUSTLA 1-3
BLOOD AND GAMES 1&2
By **King Dream**

GHOST MOB
By **Stilloan Robinson**

HARD AND RUTHLESS 1&2
MOB TOWN 251

THE BILLIONAIRE BENTLEYS 1-3
REAL G'S MOVE IN SILENCE
By **Von Diesel**

MOB TIES 1-7
SOUL OF A HUSTLER, HEART OF A KILLER 1-3
GORILLAZ IN THE TRENCHES
OOPS CRY TOO 1&2
THE DAUGHTER OF A CARTEL BOSS
By **SayNoMore**

BODYMORE MURDERLAND 1-3
THE BIRTH OF A GANGSTER 1-4
By **Delmont Player**

FOR THE LOVE OF A BOSS 1&2
By **C. D. Blue**

KILLA KOUNTY 1-5
TENDER
By **Khufu**

MOBBED UP 1-4
THE BRICK MAN 1-5
THE COCAINE PRINCESS 1-10
STEPPERS 1-3
SUPER GREMLIN 1-4
A GANGSTA'S SON
By **King Rio**

MONEY GAME 1&2
By **Smoove Dolla**

A GANGSTA'S KARMA 1-5
By **FLAME**

KING OF THE TRENCHES 1-3
By **GHOST & TRANAY ADAMS**

BAD BITCHES WIT GUNZ 1&2
PROBLEM SOLVED
By "Christopher Diesel" Hornezes

QUEEN OF THE ZOO 1&2
By **Black Migo**

GRIMEY WAYS 1-3
BETRAYAL OF A G
By **Ray Vinci**

XMAS WITH AN ATL SHOOTER
By **Ca$h & Destiny Skai**

KING KILLA 1&2
By **Vincent "Vitto" Holloway**

BETRAYAL OF A THUG 1&2
By **Fre$h**

COUNTDOWN OF A KILLA 1&2
SEX, MURDER AND GOD 1&2
GUNS DOWN, BOTTOMS UP 1&2
By Lo-Life

THE MURDER QUEENS 1-7
By **Michael Gallon**

FOR THE LOVE OF BLOOD 1-4
By **Jamel Mitchell**

HOOD CONSIGLIERE 1&2
NO TIME FOR ERROR
By **Keese**

PROTÉGÉ OF A LEGEND 1,2&3

LOVE IN THE TRENCHES 1&2
By **Corey Robinson**

THE PLUG'S RUTHLESS DAUGHTER 1&2
By **Tony Daniels**

BORN IN THE GRAVE 1-3
CRIME PAYS
By **Self Made Tay**

MOAN IN MY MOUTH
By **XTASY**

TORN BETWEEN A GANGSTER AND A GENTLEMAN
By **J-BLUNT & Miss Kim**

LOYALTY IS EVERYTHING 1-3
CITY OF SMOKE 1-3
By **Molotti**

HERE TODAY GONE TOMORROW 1&2
By **Fly Rock**

WOMEN LIE MEN LIE 1-4
FIFTY SHADES OF SNOW 1-3
STACK BEFORE YOU SPLURGE
GIRLS FALL LIKE DOMINOES
NAÏVE TO THE STREETS
By **ROY MILLIGAN**

PILLOW PRINCESS
By **S. Hawkins**

THE BUTTERFLY MAFIA 1-3
SALUTE MY SAVAGERY 1&2
By **Fumiya Payne**

THE LANE 1&2

ONCE YOU GO GANGSTA | COREY ROBINSON

By Ken-Ken Spence

THE PUSSY TRAP 1-5
By **Nene Capri**

DIRTY DNA
By **Blaque**

SANCTIFIED AND HORNY
by **XTASY**

BOOKS BY LDP'S CEO, CA$H

TRUST IN NO MAN
TRUST IN NO MAN 2

162

TRUST IN NO MAN 3
BONDED BY BLOOD
SHORTY GOT A THUG
THUGS CRY
THUGS CRY 2
THUGS CRY 3
TRUST NO BITCH
TRUST NO BITCH 2
TRUST NO BITCH 3
TIL MY CASKET DROPS
RESTRAINING ORDER
RESTRAINING ORDER 2
IN LOVE WITH A CONVICT
LIFE OF A HOOD STAR
XMAS WITH AN ATL SHOOTER

www.ingramcontent.com/pod-product-compliance
Lightning Source LLC
Chambersburg PA
CBHW060420260626
47161CB00005B/1716